WHO'S THE THIEF ON CLINTON STREET?

Just as quickly as the store had filled with people, it emptied. The old lady left too. She had bought two cans of peas. And that was it. Gaby had nothing on her. If she had slipped anything into her bag, she'd done it when Gaby wasn't looking.

"Anything?" Tina asked Gaby as she came back into the store. Gaby shook her head.

"Hey, you!" Mr. Fernandez suddenly yelled. "Stop, thief!"

Gaby turned just in time to see someone duck behind a woman carrying a baby and squeeze out the door.

"Wait!" Gaby yelled, racing for the door.

JOIN THE TEAM

Do you watch GHOSTWRITER on PBS? Then you know that when you read and write to solve a mystery or unravel a puzzle, you're using the same smarts and skills the Ghostwriter team uses.

We hope you'll join the team and read along to help solve the mysterious and puzzling goings-on in these GHOSTWRITER books!

Clinton Street Crime Wave

LABAN CARRICK HILL

ILLUSTRATIONS BY PHIL FRANKÉ

A CHILDREN'S TELEVISION WORKSHOP BOOK

BANTAM BOOKS
NEW YORK • TORONTO • LONDON • SYDNEY • AUCKLAND

CLINTON STREET CRIME WAVE
A Bantam Book / November 1994

Ghostwriter, **Ghost writer** *and* ●͡
are trademarks of Children's Television Workshop.
All rights reserved. Used under authorization.

Cover art by Susan Herr
Interior illustrations by Phil Franké

ISBN 0-553-48186-X

Published simultaneously in the United States and Canada

Bantam Books are published by Bantam Books, a division of Bantam
Doubleday Dell Publishing Group, Inc. Its trademark, consisting of the
words "Bantam Books" and the portrayal of a rooster, is Registered in U.S.
Patent and Trademark Office and in other countries. Marca Registrada.
Bantam Books, 1540 Broadway, New York, New York 10036.

PRINTED IN THE UNITED STATES OF AMERICA

CWO   0 9 8 7 6 5 4 3 2 1

CHAPTER 1

"No way."

"Way."

"No way. Really?" Hector Carrero asked. He stopped drilling and leaned on the table, staring at Alex Fernandez.

The boys were in Phil Reiner's woodworking shop on Clinton Street. Hector was helping Alex make a bookcase for Alex's sister, Gaby. It was going to be her Christmas present.

"It's true. Didn't you hear Phil on the phone?" Alex said. "He was talking to Annette about the new locks the hardware store put in this morning." Annette was Phil's wife. In exchange for using Phil's wood Alex and Hector had agreed to pass out holiday fliers for Annette's clothing store.

"You sure?" Hector asked.

"Positive. He said 'break-in.' Just like that."

"Wow." Hector lowered the drill press to the wood again. He was getting good at drilling holes perfectly halfway through the board. "Watch, no hands!" He waved his hands in the air as the drill spun into the board.

"Hey, guys," Phil called. "Stop clowning around."

"Oops," Hector said.

"Busted!" Alex whispered, chuckling.

"Oh, no!" Hector yelled as the machine suddenly took over. Before he could do anything, the drill had bored a hole clear through the wood.

Phil ran over. "You okay?"

Hector nodded, ashamed. "I'm sorry," he said to Alex.

"No sweat." Alex clapped him on the shoulder and examined the board.

"It could have been your hand that had the hole in it!" Phil scolded.

Hector looked at his shoes.

"I didn't mean to yell," Phil said, after a moment. "Listen, we'll plug the hole with a dab of putty. No one will know the difference."

Phil showed Hector how to fill the board and then had Hector try it himself.

"Phil?" Hector said as he smoothed the putty.

"Hmmm?"

"Alex says there was a break-in here last night," Hector said. "Is that true?"

"Unfortunately, he's right. When I came in this morning, most of my scrap wood was missing."

"Scrap wood?" Alex repeated.

"Yeah, the wood that's left over when I finish a project," Phil said, pointing to a pile of odd-sized pieces of wood. Some were thin and long and some were short slabs. Others had holes in them. "I save it for other projects."

"Nothing else was taken?" Alex asked.

Phil shook his head. "Nope. No tools. No good planks. Just a pile of scraps."

"That's really weird," Hector said. "How'd the thief get in?"

"I'm not sure," Phil admitted. "The shop was locked up tight as a drum when I came in this morning."

"Did you call the police?" Alex asked.

Phil shrugged. "Over a few pieces of scrap wood? What are the police going to do—laugh? I figured it wasn't worth bothering them."

Alex nodded. He could see Phil's point.

Just then there was a burst of cold air. Phil's wife, Annette, came into the shop with a paper bag filled with fliers. She waved her hand at all the sawdust floating in the air. "Looks like you guys have been working hard!"

"We're almost ready to put the bookcase together," Alex said excitedly.

"Well, you'll have to do that tomorrow," Annette said. "I've got to get these fliers out today." She dumped the bag into Alex's arms.

"Ooof!" Alex groaned. "All these today?"

"Oh, is that too much?" She asked in a way that Alex and Hector both knew that even *she* knew it was too much. The boys exchanged glances.

"Honey," Phil said, "it's getting pretty late for the boys. Maybe they should hand out those fliers tomorrow."

"Well, okay," Annette said reluctantly, looking out the window. It was getting dark out.

"Let's clean up and head home," Phil said.

Hector grabbed a broom and started working his way around the machines. The shop was crowded with equipment and supplies, but it was neat. Phil had a place for everything.

As Hector swept around the woodpile, he spotted a small red glove in a pile of sawdust. He picked it out, brushing off chips of wood. "Hey, what's this?"

Alex stopped scrubbing the drill press with a brush and went over.

"Is this anybody's?" Hector asked, looking toward Annette and Phil.

"Not likely," Phil answered. "It would only cover about three of my fingers." He held up his large, muscular hand. It was almost the size of Hector's head.

"I've never seen it before," Annette said, shaking her head.

Hector tried on the glove. It fit almost perfectly. "Maybe this is a clue to the robbery!" He handed the glove to Alex.

"Hey, there's something written on it," Alex said.

"Looks like it's embroidered," Annette said.

"Let me see," Hector said. He peered at the glove. " 'Two roads di . . . di . . . ver . . . ' "

"Diverged," Alex said. "It says: 'Two roads diverged in a wood, and I.' "

" 'And I' what?" Hector asked, confused.

"That's all it says," Alex said.

"Maybe the other glove has the rest of the sentence," Annette said. She squinted at the fliers in the bag. "Maybe I should have printed these on red or green paper," she added to Phil. "I changed the layout. Take a look and tell me what you think."

Hector was still looking at the glove. "What does it mean?" he asked Alex.

"I'm not sure," Alex said. "It's something about there being two roads going in different directions."

"In the woods?"

Suddenly a bright, glowing ball moved across the glove and lingered over the words.

"Ghostwriter!" Hector whispered.

Ghostwriter was a mysterious being that only Hector, Alex, and a few of their friends knew about. The group of kids called themselves the Ghostwriter team. Working together, they'd solved a lot of mysteries in the neighborhood.

Ghostwriter was their secret friend and helper. He couldn't see or hear, but he could communicate through writing. The team could see his words, but Ghostwriter didn't appear to anyone else except in very rare cases.

Alex glanced at Phil and Annette. They weren't paying any attention to him or Hector. He pulled out his pocket notebook. GHOSTWRITER, THERE WAS A BREAK-IN AT PHIL'S, he wrote. WE FOUND A GLOVE THAT MAY BE A CLUE.

Ghostwriter picked up some letters from off the glove and rearranged them to spell out: **STRANGE ENDING.**

THE WORDS ARE WRITTEN ON THE GLOVE, Alex wrote. WE THINK THE REST OF THE SENTENCE MAY

BE ON THE OTHER GLOVE, BUT WE DON'T KNOW WHERE IT IS.

MAYBE YOU SHOULD CHECK AROUND FOR OTHER CLUES, Ghostwriter wrote back.

"You think the other glove is somewhere in the shop?" Hector asked Alex.

"Even if it isn't, Ghostwriter's right, we should look around for other clues," Alex said. The two of them started to search the workshop.

Hector checked the windows. All of them were closed and locked.

Alex glanced at the ceiling. He started as he noticed a small window up there.

"Hey, Phil," Alex said. "There's a skylight up there." He pointed to the ceiling.

"Sure," Phil answered. "Without that skylight I'd be in the dark all the time."

Alex shook his head. That wasn't what he'd meant. "You don't think that anyone could—"

"Climb in through there?" Phil said. "No, it's so small, you'd have to be Hector to get through it."

"Hey!" Hector said, flexing his muscles. "I'm not that small."

Everyone laughed.

Hector stepped forward to get a better look at the skylight and stubbed his toe on the table saw. "Ouch!"

"Watch where you're going, tough guy, or you're going to hurt yourself," Phil said.

"You shouldn't keep things just lying around," Hector

said, holding on to his foot. "Someone could trip and break every bone in their body and have to go to the hospital and—"

"I keep the table saw under the skylight so I can use daylight to my advantage," Phil said. "And trip Hector, of course."

Annette rolled her eyes. "He built this place from scratch. I've told him a million times to have more lights installed. A simple thing, but does he listen?"

Just then the door to the shop rumbled open. CeCe Jenkins, the grandmother of Alex and Hector's friend Jamal, walked in. She delivered the mail in the neighborhood.

"Mail!" CeCe called.

"Hey, Mrs. Jenkins!" Alex and Hector said together.

"Well, what are you two doing here?" CeCe asked.

Alex explained that he was making Gaby a Christmas present. While he was talking, Ghostwriter's glow appeared and dipped into the envelope in CeCe's hand.

CeCe nodded with a smile. "Making a gift for your sister. Now, that's what this season's all about!" She handed the letter to Phil and left.

Ghostwriter zipped across Alex's notebook, writing:
TROUBLE.

Phil opened the letter. As he read it, his face suddenly grew pale. Silently he handed the letter to Annette. Alex and Hector craned over her shoulder.

PAY NOW OR PAY LATER. BUT YOU'LL PAY!
RICK

CHAPTER 2

"Whoa!" said Hector. His eyes were round.

"Who's Rick?" Alex asked.

"He does odd jobs for me once in a while," Phil said. "I had him help me out on a big job this fall. But I had to let him go last week when it was finished. He was really angry because the job ended two weeks early." Phil looked at the note again.

"Looks like he might be our suspect," Alex said.

"No," Phil said. "I can't believe Rick would break into my shop."

Annette looked seriously at her husband. "Are you sure? This note is pretty weird, arriving the day after you were burglarized—"

"Please, Annette. Rick has worked for me off and on for the past two years," Phil said stubbornly. "I just don't think he'd do something like this. Besides, how do you suppose he broke into the shop? He returned the keys the day he left."

"He could have easily made a copy of the keys," Annette argued. "Good thing you've changed the locks. That way he won't be able to do it again."

"Rick didn't break in," Phil insisted. He crumpled the note and threw it in the garbage can. "Anyway, if I know Rick, he would have taken something valuable."

Hector picked the letter out of the garbage and quickly stuffed it into his pocket.

Alex checked the new lock on the back door. "Strong lock," he said over his shoulder.

"The best," Phil said. "Paul from the hardware store put one on the front door as well."

Hector hurried over to inspect the lock. As he looked down, he noticed scuff marks at the base of the door. "Hey, here's a footprint!"

"It looks like a sneaker print," Alex said, kneeling. "Look at the swirls and circles."

"It's from the person who broke in!" Hector yelled.

Phil went over and placed his foot beside the print. Phil's boot was nearly two inches shorter. "It's too big to be mine, that's for sure," he said. "Hmm."

"It looks like Shaquille O'Neal came through this door," Alex said, staring at the print. "Man, that's a big foot!"

"Maybe we should copy the print," Hector suggested. He lifted his foot to look at the tread on his own sneaker. "Maybe if we can figure out what kind of shoe it is, we can look for people wearing that kind of sneaker."

Phil gave Hector a startled glance. "Okay, Sherlock."

"Does this guy Rick wear sneakers?" Hector asked.

"I'm not sure," Phil said thoughtfully. "It could also be the locksmith's footprint, though."

"We better call a rally," Hector whispered to Alex.

"Yeah, you're right," Alex agreed. Whipping out his notebook again, he wrote: RALLY A!

The letters lit up and then Ghostwriter was off.

I'M READY TO GIVE UP SCHOOL, Lenni Frazier wrote in her notebook. She sat slumped at a desk, staring down so that her long brown hair hung over her face.

WHAT WILL YOU DO INSTEAD? Ghostwriter wrote back.

I DON'T KNOW. I DON'T CARE! Lenni wrote. She was upset. School was hard enough already. It wasn't fair that she had to work on her history project with someone like Jade Clintock!

Lenni and Jade had been paired up by their history teacher. They had agreed twice to meet after school to get started, but both times Jade hadn't shown up. Their topic had been due on Monday. Now it was Thursday already, and there was only a week and a day left before their whole project was due. Earlier that day, when Mr. O'Connor had asked Lenni what topic she and Jade had chosen, Lenni had to tell him the truth: They hadn't.

"Lenni and Jade," Mr. O'Connor said, getting the girls' attention. "We need to talk seriously about this project. I paired you two because I thought both of you could gain from each other's strengths. But you've got to get started in order to finish!"

Lenni and Jade glanced at each other, then away.

"Lenni," Mr. O'Connor continued, "you have not done as well as I had hoped, even though you have handed in every assignment." He turned to Jade, a rail-thin girl with long dark hair in a ponytail. "And you made a high grade on the last test, but you have not turned in at least half of your assignments."

Lenni glanced over at Jade, surprised. She hadn't known Jade was so smart!

"I know doing a project with someone else can be difficult," Mr. O'Connor continued, "but both of you need to try harder to work together."

"But, Mr. O'Connor," Lenni burst out, frustrated, "how can I work with Jade when she never even shows up at our meetings?"

"I told you already. I got sick," Jade muttered.

"If I may continue," Mr. O'Connor interrupted. "This project is, at the moment, the only way for the two of you to improve your grades."

The only way not to fail, Lenni thought.

"So it's up to you two to figure it out. Remember, I want a report on an event that happened in New York City more than a hundred years ago. Use two written sources. And if you don't finish the project before holiday break, you'll have to work on it over vacation."

Lenni groaned. School was the last thing she wanted to think about on her vacation!

· 12 ·

"All right," Mr. O'Connor said, after fixing each of them with a stern look. "Get started."

Jade bolted out of her chair and hurried from the classroom. Lenni got up to follow, but when she came out, Jade was already halfway down the hall. Lenni ran to catch up. At least she knew now that Jade had done well on that killer test.

"Hey, Jade, wait up!" Lenni called.

Jade turned, flipping her hair over her shoulder.

"We have to meet. How about tomorrow right after school . . . at your house?" Lenni thought if they made plans to meet at Jade's house, there was no way Jade could duck out.

"Uh—no. My mom's sick. I can't have anyone over," Jade said quickly. Turning, she started walking toward the door again.

"Okay, how about my house?" Lenni called.

"Yeah. Sure," Jade yelled over her shoulder.

"What time?" Lenni asked. "Four o'clock?"

"Sounds good," Jade answered as she stepped through the door.

"Wait!" Lenni yelled. "I haven't told you where I—"

SLAM! The door shut.

" . . . live." Lenni finished. But Jade was gone.

CHAPTER 3

Rrrriip. Gaby Fernandez tore open a carton filled with cans of tomato paste and stamped a price on the top of each can. Mr. Fernandez had said Alex could work on some dumb project for school today, instead of pricing stock at the bodega. *It's not fair,* Gaby thought. Now she had to do twice as much work as usual.

In the next aisle over, Mr. Fernandez was also unpacking stacks of cartons.

"Díos mio." Mr. Fernandez sighed.

Gaby poked her head over the top of the shelves. "What's wrong, Papa?"

"Look at this!" Mr. Fernandez complained. "I just stocked the soup section yesterday and now there's no more chicken noodle soup."

"Maybe someone likes chicken noodle soup," Gaby suggested.

"No, I know I didn't sell ten cans of chicken soup in one day." Mr. Fernandez kicked an empty box and tore open another.

Shrugging, Gaby turned back to putting the tomato paste on the shelf.

"This is the second time in a week something's missing. Monday it was beans. Today it was soup. Tomorrow it'll probably be olives. I'm being slowly robbed of my business!" Mr. Fernandez slammed a can on the shelf, making Gaby jump.

"Did you call the police, Papa?" she asked.

"*Sí,*" Mr. Fernandez said sadly. "But the policeman says there's nothing he can do without more to go on. He says I have to catch the person in the act. The policeman also said there have been more than a few thefts like these on this block—and farther over on Clinton Street."

A fluorescent light bulb started a loud and annoying hum above their heads. Then it blew out. "*Mira!* Look!" Mr. Fernandez shouted. He took a deep breath and stared at the bulb as if it had blown out on purpose. Finally he stomped to the back of the store to get a new bulb.

Gaby continued to stock the shelves until her father returned. "Papa?"

"*Sí?*"

"Do you have any idea who's stealing from us?"

Mr. Fernandez shrugged. "*No sé.* I keep thinking it's that old lady who only buys canned peas, but when I watch her, she doesn't do anything suspicious."

"What does she look like?" Gaby asked.

Mr. Fernandez thought for a moment. "She's tiny and

kind of stooped over." He bent over to show Gaby. "And she wears the same blue housecoat every day. And she's got those stockings that go only halfway up her calves."

"Well," Gaby said, "next time, *I'll* watch her too."

"It's hard," Mr. Fernandez answered. "Sometimes she comes in the store when it's busy and I can't keep an eye on her the whole time. It's only after she's gone and the store has quieted down that I notice missing cans."

The Ghostwriter team could help, Gaby thought. They could keep their eyes peeled around the store. And they might find some clues that would lead them to the thief!

She decided she'd better call a rally. She hurried over to the cash register and scribbled on a paper bag:

RALLY G!

At almost the same time a message from Ghostwriter appeared on the bag:

RALLY A!

Gaby stared. "Huh?" she said. She scratched her head. There was a pause. Then Ghostwriter wrote:

?

At that moment Jamal Jenkins was hurrying toward the community center with Tina Nguyen at his heels.

"Slow down, Jamal." Tina panted.

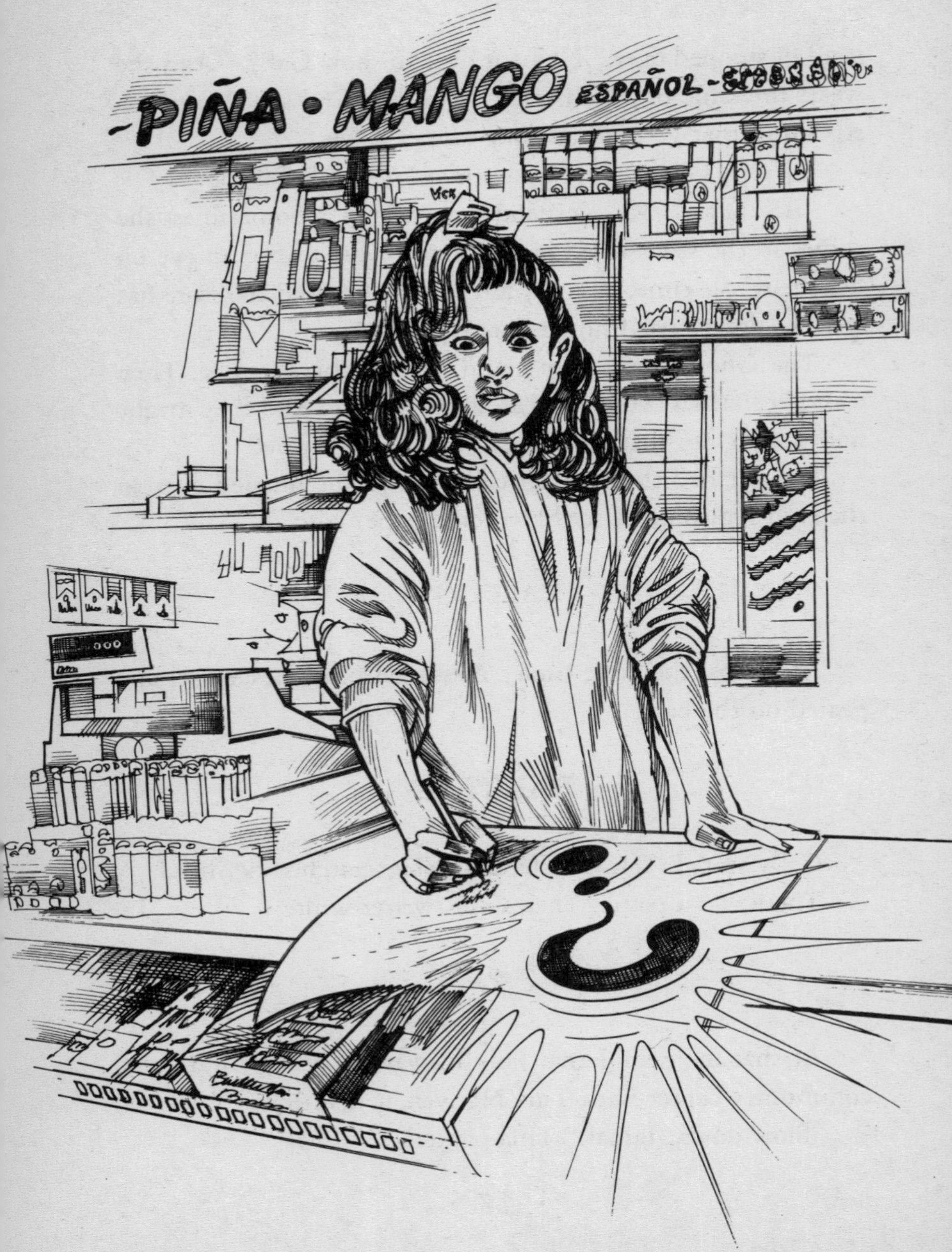
PIÑA • MANGO
ESPAÑOL

"Hurry up," Jamal said. "I want to get to the center in time to play at least three games." Tina and Jamal were heading for the video-game room. They were going to have a knock-down-drag-out Zargon battle. Tina had challenged Jamal, and he wanted to leave her in the dust.

"Look!" Tina suddenly yelled.

"What now?" Jamal turned around and saw a store advertisement spin into two floating messages:

RALLY A!
RALLY G!

When Tina and Jamal walked into Alex and Gaby's room, Lenni was sitting on the floor by a stack of magazines. Alex and Hector were on Alex's bed, both leaning against the wall. Gaby sat at her desk.

"What's up? Who called the rally?" Jamal asked.

"Yeah—I got two different messages on my way home from school," Lenni said.

"I called it," Alex and Gaby said at the same time. They faced each other with their arms folded.

"I called it first," Gaby said.

"How do you know?" Alex retorted.

"Guys, relax," Jamal said. "One at a time, okay?"

"Fine, go first then, Gaby," Alex finally muttered.

Gaby turned to the team. "Someone's stealing from the bodega."

"What?" Alex yelled. "Why didn't you say so?"

"When?" Lenni asked.

"It happened a couple of times in the last week," Gaby said. She explained how she'd been helping her dad fill the shelves when he discovered the missing soup. "The worst thing is that it isn't just a cupcake here and there. It's lots of stuff."

"I thought it just happened once!" Alex exclaimed. "We've got to stop it!"

"It must be a crime wave!" Hector said excitedly. The Clinton Street Crime Wave! "Alex and I have a theft to report too. We were—ow!"

Alex had kicked Hector to make sure he didn't spill the Christmas surprise for Gaby. Hector glanced sideways at Alex. "I wasn't going to tell," he whispered.

"Tell what?" Gaby asked.

"Nothing," Hector said quickly. "We were helping Phil out at his workshop when we found out that someone broke into his shop last night."

"I thought you were supposed to be working on a project for school," Gaby grumbled.

Alex ignored her. "We think it could have been the guy who works for Phil sometimes," he said. He told everyone about their suspect and clues.

"Let's get Ghostwriter in on this," Jamal suggested. He pulled a pen from his pocket and wrote: GW—THE BODEGA HAS BEEN ROBBED AND PHIL'S SHOP WAS ALSO BROKEN INTO!

THAT'S TERRIBLE! WHAT'S YOUR PLAN?

"Maybe we should split up to solve these crimes," Tina suggested.

Lenni jumped in. "Let's start a casebook. Write down everything we know about the bodega thefts, first."

Gaby pulled a loose-leaf notebook from under her bed. She opened it and divided the first page into two columns with a heading at the top of each. "We'll make separate columns for each case."

Tina thought for a moment and said, "We don't know much about the bodega thefts except what was stolen."

"We have a suspect, the old lady with the rolled-down stockings," Gaby said.

"And motive," Alex said.

"And what would that be, Mr. Know-it-all?" Gaby asked.

"Simple," Alex said. "The person's obviously hungry."

"Makes sense," Jamal agreed. "What else do we know?"

With pen in hand Gaby wrote as quickly as she could as everyone came up with clues.

BODEGA

Crime: 10 cans of chicken noodle soup stolen
              10 cans of kidney beans stolen
Suspect: Old lady who buys peas
Evidence: She's always in the shop before something is
              stolen.

PHIL'S WORKSHOP

Crime: Break-in
              Scrap wood stolen

Suspect:	Former employee Rick
Evidence:	Threatening note by Rick
	Giant sneaker print at back door
	Glove embroidered with *Two roads diverged in a wood, and I*

Everyone stared at the two lists.

"I'll help stake out the bodega tomorrow," Tina said to Gaby. "Sounds like you're going to need help when the store gets busy. And I bet the shoplifter will be back."

"Yeah," Gaby answered. "Friday is one of the busiest days of the week."

"Hector and I will check out Rick tomorrow," Alex said. "It looks like he's the prime suspect at Phil's shop." He really wanted to stay and guard the bodega, but he knew it was up to him and Hector to find out who had broken in at Phil's. They were the ones who had brought the case to the team in the first place.

"Maybe we should go to Myrtle Sports," Hector added. "I bet we can match the sneaker print there. If we know what the thief's shoes look like, we've got him!"

"Good thinking," Alex said.

"I'll try to figure out what *Two roads diverged in a wood, and I* means," Jamal said as he held the glove in his hand. "It sounds familiar—I think it might be from a poem. I'll look through a poetry anthology to see if I can find it."

"Poetry anthol-o . . . ?" Hector stumbled.

"Anthology," Tina explained. "It's a book full of poems by different people."

"I want to help out too," Lenni said. She sighed. "But I've got this project hanging over my head—like an ax." She drew her finger across her throat.

"Project?" Jamal said. "Maybe we can help."

"Well, it's for history. And I've got this project partner I'm supposed to be doing it with, but I don't think she cares."

"Someone we know?" Alex asked.

"I don't think so," Lenni said gloomily. "Her name's Jade Clintock, and she cuts school all the time. Anyway, we're supposed to meet tomorrow to finally get started. I just hope she shows up this time!" Lenni rolled her eyes. "If she doesn't, I'm dead meat."

"Hey, it's cool," Jamal said, patting Lenni on the shoulder. "Do what you have to do. We'll keep you posted on the cases."

"Yeah," Alex added. "Just finish that project."

"Or *I'll* be finished!" Lenni exclaimed.

CHAPTER 4

Friday after school Hector and Alex headed over to Phil's. Alex was itching to put the bookcase together. He was worried about getting it finished in time for Christmas, especially now that Gaby was getting suspicious about his taking time off from working at the bodega. Also, Mr. Fernandez was strict about Alex keeping his work schedule.

Hector was brimming with ideas about their case. He pulled the drawing of the sneaker print from his pocket. "Let's stop by Myrtle Sports on the way to Phil's."

"I don't know. We've got a lot to do."

"It'll only take a second. How many sneakers can there be?"

"Millions," Alex answered. He sighed. "But you're right. We should take care of it."

Inside Myrtle Sports a salesman asked, "Can I help you boys?"

"Uh . . . " Hector wasn't sure what to say. "I think so, but in kind of a different way than you think."

"We're looking for a certain type of sneaker," Alex added.

"Which one? We have every name brand and more."

"That's the problem," Alex said. "We're not sure."

"We have a copy of the tread, though," Hector added. He held out the paper. The salesman looked at it.

"This one's easy," he said immediately. "See these swirls and circles? It's a basketball shoe." He grabbed a large, black, bulky Slam Max high-top off the shelf. "This one." He matched the print to the sneaker. "Well, it isn't exactly the same tread, but I'd bet the print is an earlier version from a couple of years ago."

"Slam Max! They're the best," Hector said.

"One of the best," the salesman agreed.

"Do you think some other sneaker company could have the same tread?" Alex asked.

The man shook his head. "Not likely. These guys patent their treads so that it's illegal for anyone else to copy them."

Hector and Alex looked at the shoe again.

"Would you like to try the shoe on?" the salesman asked.

"Yes!" Hector wanted to say.

"No, thanks," Alex said, retreating, "but we appreciate your help." He headed out of the store with Hector following.

On the street Hector asked, "Don't you wish you had a pair like that?"

"Do I ever," Alex answered. "If it's Rick's print, he sure has good taste!"

The same afternoon Lenni waited on the steps of Hurston for Jade to come out. Jade hadn't shown up at class, but Lenni still hoped she could catch her leaving school.

While she waited, she wrote to Ghostwriter:

I'M FLUNKING HIS

Just then a group of students came out of the building. Lenni stopped writing to look at them. They were all wrapped up against the cold, but even so she could see that Jade wasn't among them. She turned back to her notebook, disappointed.

STORY, she continued writing. IT'S SO BORING. IT'S JUST A BUNCH OF DATES. I CAN NEVER REMEMBER WHAT HAPPENED WHEN.

Ghostwriter answered: **HIS STORY? OR YOURS?**

"Huh?" Then Lenni realized that she had spelled *history* with one too many *S*'s. HISTORY. NOT HIS STORY, she wrote. But then she looked closely at the word *history*.

GW, DO YOU THINK THE WORD *HISTORY* FIRST CAME FROM SOMEONE TELLING A STORY?

IT SEEMS LIKELY.

THAT'S COOL. IF I COULD JUST TELL A STORY, THIS PROJECT WOULD BE EASY.

MAYBE YOU CAN.

I DON'T KNOW ABOUT THAT, Lenni wrote. MY PROJECT HAS TO BE ON SOMETHING THAT HAPPENED A HUNDRED YEARS AGO IN NEW YORK.

CHOOSE SOMETHING YOU CARE ABOUT, Ghostwriter advised. **THEN THINGS WILL FALL INTO PLACE.**

Lenni thought for a minute. I CARE ABOUT MUSIC. AND SINGING.

MUSIC HAS A STORY, Ghostwriter wrote, DOESN'T IT?

I HOPE SO! Lenni wrote. BECAUSE MUSIC'S THE STORY I WANT TO TALK ABOUT.

SOUNDS GOOD TO ME!

Lenni checked her watch. It had been over half an hour. Jade wasn't going to show. Lenni sighed. Maybe she would have to do this project on her own.

Thump. Thump. Out of breath, Hector banged hard on the door to Phil's shop. It was cold and his hand stung. Then he noticed a piece of paper taped to the door.

"What's that?" Alex asked.

"A note from Phil."

Friday, 3:00 P.M.

Hi, guys!

Sorry, but I've got to cancel today. I'm going out to Long Island to pick out some cherry boards and I won't get back until late. Can you come tomorrow? I'll be in the shop all day.

Phil

As they read it, the note began to glow. Ghostwriter was reading it too.

"Ghostwriter," Hector said. He dug a pen out of his pocket and handed it to Alex.

Alex wrote: WE WERE GOING TO ASK PHIL WHERE RICK LIVED, BUT HE'S NOT HERE.

Hector took the pen from Alex and wrote: WE WANT TO CATCH THIS GUY BEFORE HE BREAKS INTO THE SHOP AGAIN.

DO YOU KNOW RICK'S LAST NAME? Ghostwriter wrote.

Alex took the pen. WE WISH! IF WE DID, WE COULD HAVE LOOKED IN THE PHONE BOOK.

TOO BAD, Ghostwriter answered. **ANY OTHER CLUES?**

ALL WE HAVE IS THE NOTE HE SENT TO PHIL, Alex wrote.

Hector pulled the note from his pocket and read it again. Ghostwriter read along. At the bottom of the paper Ghostwriter's glow suddenly paused.

That's when Alex noticed the letterhead.

"Look!" He pointed it out to Hector. "The note is on stationery!"

"And the stationery has an address!" Hector crowed.

GW, Alex wrote, I THINK WE FOUND IT. MARCY RESIDENCE HOTEL.

CHECK THERE, Ghostwriter wrote.

"Five sixty Waverly Street," Alex read out loud. "We're there!"

At the Marcy Residence Hotel, Alex and Hector walked into the sparse lobby. It had shabby, worn carpets and stained walls. At the desk the clerk sat with his back to the lobby as he watched TV. Hector cleared his throat to get his attention, but it didn't work.

"Do you have someone named Rick staying here?" Alex finally asked.

The man turned to look with a frown. "Who wants to know?"

"Well," Alex said. He looked at Hector. They should have made a plan before they came. "Well, I—um—I have a few questions to ask him about some work he's done," Alex said at last. He wondered how much he should say.

"What kind of work?"

"A job for Phil Reiner," Alex answered. "Rick works for him sometimes."

The man looked at Alex and didn't answer. Alex nervously pushed a strand of hair off his forehead.

"We've just got a few questions. It's for our school paper," Hector said. "Phil said Rick was a real whiz at fixing things and would be a good person to interview."

The man thought about that for a minute and stood up. He towered so far over Alex and Hector that they had to take a step back. "I'm Rick. What do you want to know?"

"You—you work here?" Alex said with a gulp. He stared at the muscles in Rick's arms.

"Yeah," Rick said. "What's it to you?"

"Have you been working with Phil for a long time?"

"Until he cheated me out of some work he promised me," Rick said. His eyes narrowed and he stared hard at Alex. "I got this gig now."

Just then the phone behind him rang. Rick answered it. He sat back into his chair and propped his feet onto the desk. Hector hit Alex on the arm and pointed. Rick had big feet. Huge.

Alex nodded, excited.

"So," he said after Rick hung up the phone, "—you work out a lot?"

"Some," Rick answered. "Not as much as I used to. Don't have the time or the money."

"You must play a lot of basketball, huh?" Hector asked.

Rick gave Hector a strange look but then laughed. "What do you care? You a scout for the Knicks or something?"

"Uh, no," Hector said. "I . . . uh . . . wanted to get a pair of basketball sneakers, and I was going to ask you what's the best for hoops."

"Oh, really?" Rick asked suspiciously, as he looked from Alex to Hector.

The phone rang again and Rick picked it up.

"Listen, kids," he said with his hand over the receiver, "I'd like to help you and all, but I'm busy."

"But—" Alex started to say.

"Beat it," Rick growled. He whirled to face the wall and continued talking on the phone.

Outside, Hector was practically jumping up and down. "Did you see his feet?" he kept yelling. "Did you?"

"Yeah," Alex said. "They were massive. I don't think I've ever seen feet so large."

"He wasn't wearing shoes," Hector said.

"He probably can't find any that fit," Alex responded.

They both laughed and headed down the street.

"I just wish we could have seen him with sneakers on," Hector said. "How do we know for sure if he owns a pair of Slam Max?"

"We don't," Alex replied. "And we still need to check the locksmith's feet, too, on our way home. We'd better be absolutely sure about this guy Rick before we accuse him of anything."

"Yeah," Hector said. "It would be a bad idea to come up against Rick without proof. He could turn us into pretzels if he wanted to."

At the hardware store a short guy stood over a grinding machine working on a set of keys. He had a thin mustache and wore a Mets cap low over his brow.

"That can't be the guy who made the footprints at Phil's shop," Alex whispered.

"Right," Hector agreed. Then, after a moment, he asked, "Why?"

"Look how short he is," Alex said. "There's no way such a short person could be such a bigfoot."

"Oh, yeah," Hector said, chuckling. "He is pretty short, isn't he?"

"Can I help you?" the man asked.

"Um, excuse me—we're friends of Phil who owns the woodworking shop a few blocks down—and we were wondering if you were the locksmith who changed his locks yesterday morning?"

"Sure am," he said. "Can I help you?"

"No, thanks," Alex said quickly. He grabbed Hector's arm and pulled him out the door.

Outside, Alex and Hector jumped in the air for a high five.

"Yes!" Hector yelled. "Rick's our man!"

CHAPTER 5

Gaby lingered at the back of the bodega, rearranging boxes of detergent on the shelves. Out of the corner of her eye she was watching an old lady in a blue housedress. She wore rolled-down stockings and she walked with her shoulders hunched as if she were bending down. Gaby tried to shadow her without being noticed.

Tina hung out by Gaby, rearranging a stack of sponges. Then a crowd of people swarmed into the store.

"Yikes! I'll take the front," Tina called as she darted up an aisle toward the fruit bins.

"Fine," Gaby answered, as she hung back.

Just as quickly as the store had filled with people, it emptied. The old lady left too. She had bought two cans of peas. And that was it. Gaby had nothing on her. If she had slipped anything into her bag, she'd done it when Gaby wasn't looking.

"Anything?" Tina asked Gaby as she came back into the store. Gaby shook her head.

"Hey, you!" Mr. Fernandez suddenly yelled. "Stop, thief!"

Gaby turned just in time to see someone duck behind a woman carrying a baby and squeeze out the door.

"Wait!" Gaby yelled, racing for the door.

"Should we tell Phil about Rick?" Hector asked.

"I think so," Alex said. "We've got to be right about him. He's got to be our thief."

"Yeah," Hector agreed. "He was so mean!"

It was colder this morning than it had been yesterday. Alex and Hector were headed to Phil's shop to put the bookcase together.

When they entered the shop, Phil was piecing together a cabinet. "Just a second, guys," he said absently.

After a few minutes he stopped and wiped his hands on an old rag. "Well, I've got bad news all around. First, you can assemble the bookcase, but it's too cold today to put the finish on."

Both Alex and Hector were disappointed. They had chosen a dark cherry finish and wanted to see how it would look.

"You can do the first coat tomorrow before you hand out fliers for Annette," Phil promised.

"Okay," Alex said. "What's the other bad news?"

Phil's face darkened. "My shop was broken into again last night. This time the thief took about two hundred dollars' worth of wood. Most of the cherry boards I picked up yesterday. I need that wood to finish a desk a client ordered." He lifted a board stamped HAMMOND LUMBER and punched it angrily. Alex and Hector took a step back.

"Wood like that?" Hector asked.

"Yep. There are only a few boards left," Phil answered. "Now I have to waste the whole day making another trip out to Hammond Lumber. And, boy, are those good boards expensive!"

"But I thought you changed the locks," Alex said.

"I did," Phil said. "So who knows how the thief got in? At least none of my tools were stolen. The police told me I should install an alarm system before I walk in some morning and the workshop is bare."

"Did the police find any clues to how the person got in?" Hector asked.

Phil jiggled the front-door handle. "They said someone must have picked one of these supposedly pickproof new locks," he said. "That, or a mouse knows how to get in through the skylight and steal stuff." He picked up a ruler and chucked it into a toolbox.

The boys gazed up at the skylight. After a moment Hector said, "Alex, *dame la mano*. I want to climb up there."

Alex climbed onto the work table and boosted Hector up to the ceiling. Hector pushed the skylight open. "It's not locked."

"Can you climb through?" Alex asked.

"I think so," Hector answered. He struggled for a second, then popped through.

"I can't make it," Alex called from below. "My shoulders won't go through that little hole."

"I'm out. But there's not much of a view!" Hector yelled down. He took a cautious step forward. Cold wind ruffled his hair.

"Why not?" Alex shouted back.

"The building's surrounded."

"By what?" Alex asked.

"Other buildings," Hector told Alex. "They're all boarded up."

"Abandoned?" Alex asked. "Can you climb over to the next roof?"

"No way," Hector answered. "They're all three windows higher."

"You mean stories?" Alex asked.

"Yeah," Hector answered. He walked to the edge of roof and looked in one of the windows that wasn't boarded over. It was so close, he could almost reach across to touch the windowpane. Inside, he could see the coils in a box-spring mattress and a broken mirror against a wall.

"Hector!" Alex yelled.

That's when Hector accidentally kicked a pebble over the edge of the roof. It clattered into the alley below. Hector watched it fall, and gulped.

Phil's building looked pretty low when you were looking from the ground up. But not the other way around. The pebble clanked against a garbage Dumpster and then onto the cement pavement.

Hector bolted away from the edge and quickly climbed down into the shop.

"What did you see?" Alex asked.

Hector shrugged. "There are only abandoned buildings."

"You think someone could have gotten in from one of them?"

Hector thought about the pebble and the sound it made when it fell. It was a long scary drop to the ground. "No way. No way at all!"

Lenni lay on the floor with her headphones on as she skimmed her history book. Something about Saturday mornings made it hard to do schoolwork. It was gray and cold outside, but Lenni wished she could be out there.

Suddenly the words on the page lit up and began to spin. Ghostwriter was there.

HOW ARE YOU? he wrote.

Lenni picked up a pencil from the coffee table and wrote:

HI, GW. I'M TRYING TO WORK ON MY OWN LIKE WE TALKED ABOUT, BUT I'M STUCK. I NEED JADE'S HELP. THE TROUBLE IS, I DON'T THINK SHE CARES WHETHER SHE PASSES OR NOT.

I'LL HELP IF I CAN, Ghostwriter told her. **ISN'T THERE ANYTHING ABOUT MUSIC IN YOUR HISTORY BOOK?**

ACTUALLY, THERE IS A LOT, Lenni wrote. LIKE OPERA. BUT THAT'S BORING AND NOW I'M NOT SO SURE WHAT MUSIC HAS TO DO WITH HISTORY, ANYWAY.

MUSIC HAS BEEN AROUND SINCE THE BEGINNING OF TIME, Ghostwriter wrote.

Lenni thought for a moment. YOU'RE RIGHT. I BET I

COULD FIND SOMETHING BESIDES "THE BEGIN-
NINGS OF THE METROPOLITAN OPERA." KNOW
WHAT? IF I LIVED BACK THEN, I WOULD HAVE
SHOWN THEM SOME REAL MUSIC!

**YOU WILL MAKE HISTORY WITH YOUR MU-
SIC SOMEDAY.**

YEAH! ONE DAY I'M GOING TO BE A FAMOUS
SONGWRITER. AND MAYBE SOMEONE WILL BE DO-
ING THEIR PROJECT ON ME!

I HAVE FAITH IN YOU.

THANKS, GW, Lenni wrote. THAT MAKES ME FEEL
GOOD!

Just as she was turning back to her history book, Lenni
heard Mr. Fernandez and Gaby shouting out in front of the
bodega. She rushed down the stairs and hurried outside.

When she burst onto the street, she saw Mr. Fernandez
dragging someone by the arm. She could tell he was furious,
but she couldn't see who he was yelling at.

As Lenni approached, Mr. Fernandez stepped out of the
way. Lenni suddenly locked eyes with—

Jade!

"Now what?" Hector asked Alex, as they left Phil's shop
and headed toward Hector's house.

"I don't know," Alex said. "We're back to square one."

"Maybe," Hector said. "It sure looks like our only suspect
just got blown out of the water."

"Right," Alex agreed. "Rick couldn't have broken in this
time, 'cause the locks were changed yesterday."

Hector scowled. "But the shoe print had to have been Rick's. No one else could have feet like that," he argued. "Maybe Rick knows how to pick locks. Maybe that's what he really does, picks locks and breaks into places, and he's just worked for Phil as a cover."

Alex looked doubtful. "Well . . ."

"Yeah," Hector said. He was starting to get excited again. "That must be it! Let's go ask the locksmith if those new locks can be picked."

"But the hardware store is in the other direction from your house," Alex argued. He hated to backtrack.

"It's only one block," Hector pointed out.

Alex shrugged. It was unlikely, but he knew they should check it out.

At the hardware store a second time, Alex and Hector headed straight toward the locksmith.

The guy gave a thin smile when he saw them. "Back again? Can I help you with anything this time around?"

"Yeah," Hector said with a smile, "I think you can."

Alex explained how someone had broken into Phil's shop again. After he finished talking, the locksmith shook his head.

"No, those locks are heavy duty," he said. "It would take a real pro to pick those locks open."

"Pro, huh?" Alex said, glancing at Hector. Maybe Hector's idea was right after all!

"Maybe. But let me show you one of these locks. They're really secure." The locksmith ducked to search the shelf under the counter.

"Here," he said at last, handing over the lock. Alex and

Hector examined it. The short, wiry locksmith stepped around to show how it worked.

That's when they saw his feet. His huge feet. And the sneakers he was wearing.

Slam Max! The bigfoot they were looking for!

CHAPTER 6

"Eee-yaaaa!" Mr. Fernandez clutched Jade by her arm. "I saw you put those noodles in your backpack!"

"Wait, Mr. Fernandez," Lenni called, "there's been a mistake. Jade wouldn't—"

Mr. Fernandez snatched the backpack off Jade's shoulders. Lenni edged her way to the front of the crowd, next to Gaby and Tina. She was starting to get a sick feeling in her stomach.

"I know her," Lenni protested. "She's in my class!"

"Her?" Gaby said, pointing at Jade. "They should throw her out of school. She's a thief!"

"Don't you know better than to steal, little girl?" Mr. Fernandez demanded.

Jade just stared at him.

"What's your name?" he asked.

"Jade," she answered sullenly.

"Where do you live?"

"Around."

"Where?" he asked again.

"Around," Jade repeated, a little louder.

Scowling, Mr. Fernandez emptied the knapsack onto the sidewalk. Out fell pencils, an eraser, a notebook, and a couple of books. There were no noodles.

Mr. Fernandez looked shocked. A murmur ran through the crowd.

"Are you sure you saw her take those noodles?" Lenni asked Mr. Fernandez in a whisper. Gaby looked questioningly at her father.

"See? I didn't steal anything!" Jade shouted. She shook loose and stuffed her things back into her bag.

"I want your mother here this evening or I will report you to the police," Mr. Fernandez said firmly.

"I don't have a mother!" Jade yelled. She ran down the street.

Gaby was ready to chase her.

"No," Mr. Fernandez said, sounding sad all of a sudden. "Let her go." He shook his head. *"Ay, yo no sé—*she's just a little girl!"

The subway jolted to a stop, almost throwing Jamal out of his seat. A woman stepped on his foot and then nearly fell into his lap.

"Sorry," she said, her face turning as red as a tomato.

"No problem," Jamal groaned, trying to sound polite. Even through his thick leather high-tops he could feel the dent where the chunky heel of her shoe had dug into his foot.

He cleared the library books from the seat next to him so she could sit down. The woman thanked him and dropped down. Tucking his feet farther under the bench, Jamal opened the poetry anthology on his lap.

The subway was stalled in the middle of the Manhattan Bridge, high above the East River. It seemed likely that the train wasn't going anywhere for a while. "Come on! Let's get going!" someone muttered.

Jamal felt impatient, too, but for a different reason. He sighed. Would he have to read through all six of the thick books he'd taken out of the library, just to find one short line of poetry? There must be a thousand poems in those books— and that was only a tiny fraction of the poetry that had ever been written. There must be *millions* of poems out there. And he was looking for one short line?

I'll never *find it!* he thought.

In his notebook he had written the line from the glove: *Two roads diverged in a wood, and I*

And I what? Jamal wondered.

Suddenly the letters started to glow. Jamal smiled. Ghostwriter was there and reading along.

HI, GHOSTWRITER! he wrote.

HELLO—WHAT HAVE YOU FOUND? Ghostwriter asked.

NOTHING YET, Jamal replied. I TOOK OUT SOME POETRY BOOKS TO SEE IF I COULD FIND WHICH ONE THE LINE CAME FROM. BUT THERE'S SO MUCH TO READ THROUGH!

I'LL HELP, Ghostwriter wrote back, BUT IT IS A LOT

OF WORK! *TWO ROADS DIVERGED IN A WOOD, AND I*—THESE ARE OUR ONLY CLUES?

Suddenly Jamal had an idea. MAYBE THERE'S A FASTER WAY, he wrote. IF WE CHECK THROUGH THE TABLE OF CONTENTS, ONE OF THE WORDS FROM THE LINE MIGHT BE THERE AS PART OF THE POEM'S TITLE!

GREAT IDEA! Ghostwriter responded.

I'LL TRY THE WORD *ROAD* FIRST.

Jamal flipped to the table of contents and scanned the lists of titles with his finger. Ghostwriter followed down each page, lighting up the words as he went.

"Here's one," Jamal said aloud. " 'Ode on a Road.' " He smiled quickly at the woman next to him, who gave him a funny look. "Just talking to myself," he told her.

But when Jamal turned to "Ode on a Road," he could see immediately that it wasn't the right poem. It didn't say anything about woods. It was about a superhighway.

Sighing, he moved on to the next book. As he opened it to the contents page, Ghostwriter's glow highlighted a title halfway down the page.

" 'The Road Not Taken' by Robert Frost," Jamal read. "Let's give it a try." He turned to page 536, and quickly skimmed down the rest of the poem until he got to the last verse. And there it was. The line he was looking for!

Two roads diverged in a wood, and I—
I took the one less traveled by,
And that has made all the difference.

"Yes!" Jamal shot out of his seat and punched his fist into the air. The lady next to him shrank away, looking very worried.

Jamal was too excited to be embarrassed. He sat back down. WE'VE GOT IT! he wrote to Ghostwriter.

BEAUTIFUL WORDS! Ghostwriter wrote back.

Jamal studied the poem. Ghostwriter was right—it was beautiful, if you took the time to try to figure out what it meant. I THINK I GET IT. THIS GUY HAD A CHOICE OF TWO WAYS TO GO, he wrote. AND HE CHOSE THE ONE THAT MOST PEOPLE DON'T CHOOSE. KIND OF LIKE DOING WHAT YOU THINK IS RIGHT AND NOT WHAT EVERYONE ELSE THINKS IS RIGHT. AND THAT MADE A DIFFERENCE. THAT MADE IT BETTER.

YES, Ghostwriter wrote.

AND "I TOOK THE ONE LESS TRAVELED BY" MUST BE WHAT'S ON THE OTHER GLOVE!

YES!

GW, CAN YOU FIND THAT LINE ALL BY ITSELF? THAT'S HOW IT WILL APPEAR ON THE OTHER GLOVE. AND THEN READ WHAT'S AROUND IT. MAYBE WE CAN CRACK THIS CASE!

I'M ON THE JOB! With that Ghostwriter zipped off.

Soon the train started again. Stop after stop went by, but Ghostwriter still hadn't returned. *What's taking him so long?* Jamal wondered. His stop was next.

Finally Ghostwriter came back. **I FOUND IT. HAM- MOND LUMBER NEARBY,** he wrote.

Jamal stared. "Hammond Lumber," he repeated to himself. DO YOU THINK THAT'S FROM THE WOOD THAT WAS STOLEN FROM PHIL'S WORKSHOP? he asked Ghostwriter.

POSSIBLY.

Jamal thought about it for a minute. I THINK WE'RE ON TO SOMETHING BIG, he wrote.

The train pulled into the station. But Jamal was so busy scribbling, he almost forgot to get off.

RALLY J!!!

CHAPTER 7

"I think stealing is bad and Jade should go to jail," Gaby said. She was in her room with Tina.

Tina frowned. "But you saw for yourself, Gaby, your dad didn't find anything in her bag except school stuff."

"Yeah, but he says he's sure. My father wouldn't lie."

"Maybe he made a mistake."

Gaby was silent for a minute. "I watched that old lady like a hawk. It has to be someone!"

"But it doesn't have to be Jade! Lenni was right. Just because Jade skips school, it doesn't mean she steals too."

"I still say she's a suspect," Gaby said, writing Jade's name in the casebook. "And if she's the one who's been stealing from us, I'm going to get her!"

Just then Ghostwriter zipped across the casebook, rearranging the letters on the page to spell out:

RALLY J!!!

Lenni was in Joe's Pizza, about to bite into a steaming slice, when Ghostwriter appeared and wrote:

RALLY J!!!

Lenni grabbed her slice and wrapped it up to go. She was about to head out the door when she spotted Jade cutting across the street. Thinking fast, Lenni ducked back into Joe's Pizza and pulled her notebook and pen from her jacket.

I FOUND JADE! Lenni scribbled to Ghostwriter. I HAVE TO TALK TO HER!

ABOUT THE PROJECT? Ghostwriter asked. OR ABOUT THE TROUBLE AT THE BODEGA?

BOTH, Lenni wrote. IT'S ALL SO WEIRD! DID SHE REALLY STEAL THOSE NOODLES? IF SHE DID, WHY? I WANT TO ASK WHAT'S UP WITH HER. ALL I KNOW IS, SHE'S GOT PROBLEMS!

Ghostwriter wrote, IF SHE HAS PROBLEMS, MAYBE A FRIEND CAN HELP HER SOLVE THEM.

Lenni bit her lip. She wasn't so sure she could help. Or that she even wanted to.

She took another look out the window. Jade had almost disappeared down the block.

SHE'S LEAVING! I HAVE TO CATCH UP—THIS IS MY ONLY CHANCE! I'LL GET TO THE RALLY AS SOON AS I CAN, GW!

Lenni stuffed her notebook into her jacket and ran.

"Okay, let's face it," Alex muttered. "Rick's off the list. It looks like he really couldn't have picked that lock. And anyway, the footprint was the only evidence we had that he was in the shop."

The boys walked away from the hardware store. Hector nodded, downcast. "And now we know the footprint isn't his."

Just then Ghostwriter appeared, scrambling the letters on the side of a moving van to spell:

RALLY J!!!

"Maybe Jamal came up with some new evidence!" Alex clapped his hands together. "Let's go!"

As the boys walked quickly down the street, Hector said, "But if the thief didn't pick the lock, how *did* he get in?"

Alex spread out his hands and shrugged. "There's only one other way into the building. He must have come through the skylight."

"But we already know the skylight's too small for anyone to get through," Hector started to argue. Then he suddenly realized what Alex was saying. His eyes grew round. "Anyone . . . who's bigger than me," he said slowly.

"Right," Alex agreed. "I think our thief must be either a kid or a *very* little adult."

Hector thought about that. Then he started to giggle.

"What's so funny?" Alex asked.

"Nothing—I was just picturing Rick trying to squeeze through that little hole and getting stuck!" He sucked in his cheeks.

"He couldn't even get a foot through!" Alex laughed.

"Keep a lookout for a bigfoot climbing up these buildings with suction cups for feet!" Hector added.

"Suction cups!" Alex hooted. "Maybe he tied plungers to his feet!"

They walked past Phil's shop. When they stopped laughing, Alex said, "Seriously, though, we'd better scope out the buildings on this block. The thief had to have climbed a fire escape or something to get over to the shop."

They passed an abandoned building. Hector peered in. The door was missing and he could see clear through the empty rooms to a broken window in back. Trash and broken bottles covered the floor. A staircase led up into darkness.

"That place gives me the creeps," Hector said. "I wouldn't go into one of those abandoned buildings if you paid me."

"Me neither," Alex said. Then his eyes lit up. "But maybe someone else would."

Hector looked at Alex as if he were crazy. "No way, man—" he started to say. But then he saw what Alex meant. "Maybe the person didn't get to the roof from the outside of these buildings, but from the inside!"

"My thoughts exactly," Alex said, the way it was always said in detective books. He and Hector slapped their palms together. "We'll check it out later, after the rally. Come on, let's hurry."

"Right," Hector said. He felt proud that he'd been able

to help figure things out the way he did. They headed around the corner toward Jamal's.

Suddenly, out of nowhere, *bang!* Hector smashed into someone else! He and the other person went down in a jumble of flailing arms and legs.

"Ow!" a familiar voice complained. "Watch where you're going!"

"Lenni!" Hector gasped. "What are you doing here?"

Lenni sat up, rubbing her shoulder. "What am I doing here? What are *you* doing here?" she asked. "You almost gave me a heart attack. Why aren't you at the rally?"

"We're on our way there. Why aren't *you* at the rally?" Alex wanted to know.

Lenni took a breath. "I told Ghostwriter I'd be there as soon as I could. I'm following Jade, my project partner. I was staying far back so she wouldn't spot me, but now it looks like I lost her. She turned this corner just a minute ago. Did you see her?"

Both Hector and Alex shook their heads.

"Nah—and we walked all the way up this block. We didn't see anyone. She didn't come this way," Hector said.

"But she did," Lenni insisted. She peered down the empty street. "She couldn't have gone into one of these buildings— they're all boarded up. So how could she just disappear?"

"Doo-doo-doo-doo," Alex sang in a spooky voice. "Welcome to the Twilight Zone!"

Just then, all the parking signs along the street started to flash:

RALLY J!!! RALLY J!!!

"We're late!"

"The rally!"

"Let's go!"

Tina, Gaby, and Jamal were waiting in Jamal's room when Lenni, Alex, and Hector came in.

"What's the news?" Alex asked.

"First of all, I found the line from the glove in a poem," Jamal said. He opened the book of poetry and found the page. Everybody looked over his shoulder and read the poem.

"Then I asked Ghostwriter if he could find the other glove with *I took the one less traveled by*," Jamal went on.

"Did he find anything?" Tina asked.

"Get this," Jamal said. "Ghostwriter found *Hammond Lumber*."

"That's it! That's our wood!" Hector yelled. "Phil's wood, I mean."

"Yeah," Alex added. "From the cherry boards that were taken."

"I thought so," Jamal said. "So now we know that whoever owns this glove is the person who's been stealing from Phil."

"It fits," Alex said excitedly. "The glove is small. And Hector and I figured out that the person has to be small enough to fit through a little skylight." He and Hector explained the new clues they had.

"And," Hector added, "we think the person could have

· 57 ·

gone through one of the abandoned buildings on the block to get to Phil's roof."

"Hey, isn't it kind of a strange coincidence that Jade disappeared right around there?" Lenni asked suddenly.

"It was definitely a strange coincidence crashing into you," Alex said to Lenni. "Don't you think, Hector?"

"My nose definitely does," Hector said, rubbing his nose. "See the bump?"

Lenni laughed. "Sorry."

"Why is it strange?" Jamal wanted to know.

"Well, it just seems like she's sort of . . . around . . . for both our cases," Lenni said.

"Hey, these guys don't know what happened at the bodega this morning!" Tina pointed out.

"What happened?" Alex demanded.

Gaby told the boys how Mr. Fernandez had accused Jade of stealing. As she talked, Lenni started to wonder. Jade at the bodega . . . Jade disappearing right near Phil's workshop . . .

Could there be a connection?

Obviously, the same thought was occurring to Jamal. "We need to update the casebook," he said when Gaby was done. "It's time for another look at the clues."

"Okay." Gaby pulled the black notebook out from under her bed and the team crowded around to study it.

BODEGA

Crime: 10 cans of chicken noodle soup stolen
                    10 cans of kidney beans stolen
                    Spaghetti stolen?

Suspects: Old lady who buys peas
                    Jade

Evidence: Old lady always in the shop before
                        something is stolen.
                    Papa thinks Jade stole spaghetti.

PHIL'S WORKSHOP

Crime: Break-in
                    Scrap wood stolen
                    $200 worth of cherry planks stolen

Suspect: Former employee Rick

Evidence: Threatening note by Rick
                    Giant sneaker print at back door—
                      Locksmith's footprint
                    Glove embroidered with *Two roads diverged*
                      in a wood, and I

"Maybe Ghostwriter can help us learn more about the woodshop thief. Let's ask him if he can find any other clues near the glove," Tina suggested.

Gaby picked up her pen. GW, PLEASE LOOK FOR ANYTHING ELSE NEAR THE GLOVE YOU FOUND.

Ghostwriter's glow zipped across the page and disappeared. In a moment, though, he was back. His glow looked agitated. I *JUST FOUND IT!* he wrote.

FOUND WHAT? Gaby asked.

Ghostwriter grabbed letters and spelled out:

A—
JADE CLINTOCK
AMERICAN HISTORY

CHAPTER 8

"Jade!" Lenni screamed.

"I knew it," Gaby said. "I knew it all along! Papa was right about her!"

"There's still no proof she stole from the bodega," Jamal pointed out.

"But she's a thief! That's all I need to know," Gaby muttered.

"No wonder we bumped into each other," Alex exclaimed, looking at Lenni. "She probably saw you following her and disappeared into one of those buildings. She must know her way around them."

"This is crazy," Tina said. "Why would she go through all that trouble just to steal scrap wood?"

"Cherry boards too," Hector added.

"Whatever," Tina said. "Why wood?"

"Well, why spaghetti?" Jamal asked.

"How do you think she could have gotten into Phil's shop?" Lenni asked. "She's skinnier than Hector, so she's small enough to go through the skylight, but how could she get onto the roof?"

Hector thought of all he had seen while on Phil's roof. There was a window level with the roof that wasn't boarded up, but there was also a long fall to the ground. Still . . .

"I have an idea," he said slowly. "Maybe she jumped over from the window of one of those buildings."

"I don't see what the problem is," Gaby said. "If a thief wanted something, they'd find a way."

"I don't know," Tina said, shaking her head. "I don't see any motive. If she was going to steal stuff, wouldn't she steal something more valuable?"

"It already doesn't make sense to steal," Gaby answered. "So why would what she steals make sense?"

Jamal shook his head. "People usually do things for a reason."

Everyone thought for a moment.

"You don't think . . . " Lenni started to say. She hesitated, then went on, "You don't think that Jade lives in one of those buildings, do you?" She looked up at everyone.

"In one of those abandoned buildings?" Hector asked.

Tina bit her lip. "If she does, maybe she needed wood to burn. Maybe it's cold in that place."

Gaby remembered how Alex had joked about someone stealing because they were hungry. Maybe he was right.

"And she took the spaghetti because she was hungry?" she asked, looking over at Alex.

"She never would tell me where she lived," Lenni murmured. "I tried to get her address so I could go there to meet with her, but she told me her mother was sick. Then she told Mr. Fernandez she didn't *have* a mother." Lenni looked stricken. "Maybe she acted like that because—because she doesn't have a real home."

"This is all starting to make sense," Jamal said.

"You don't think she really lives in one of those, do you?" Gaby asked everyone.

Lenni gathered her thoughts. "I think we need to find out for sure. Let's see if we can pick up her trail later."

Gaby and Jamal crouched behind a stoop around the corner from Phil's shop. Tina, Alex, and Hector hid behind a stoop facing them.

All was quiet on the street. An old lady with a shopping cart pushed her groceries to her building. She went so slowly that Gaby almost couldn't resist jumping out from behind the stoop to help her. A gas truck rumbled by and then a few cars, but no Jade. Or Lenni, who was supposed to be following her again today.

"Maybe Jade lives in that one." Hector pointed to a building.

"No, it's got to be that one," Alex said, pointing to a run-down town house. "That's the one with the window that wasn't boarded up, right?"

"We won't know until Jade shows up," Jamal said.

"And Lenni," Gaby said.

Jamal chuckled. "Yeah, Lenni should make it back sooner

or later. She was positive that Jade would ditch her again and then make a run for home."

The team went over to investigate the town house. Suddenly Tina tugged at Alex's sleeve. "It's Jade!"

"Where?" Alex asked.

"Down the street." Hector pointed.

Jade was hurrying around the corner across the street with her head tucked into the collar of her light jacket. Hector held his breath as the team ducked behind a nearby stoop. The team wasn't very well hidden. Would she spot them?

Suddenly Jade stopped, checked up and down the street to make sure the coast was clear, and then darted down the steps into the doorway of the town house Alex had pointed out. Pulling aside a sheet of metal that covered the entrance, she slipped inside and was gone.

"Phew," Tina whispered, "that was close."

"What happened to Lenni?" Jamal muttered.

Twenty seconds later Lenni turned the corner toward the team. Gaby jumped out from behind the stoop and waved her arms. Lenni jogged over.

"What took you so long?" Tina asked. Lenni tried to catch her breath.

"Where is she?" Lenni finally said. Tina pointed to the abandoned brownstone in front of them. Lenni braced her hands on her knees, breathing hard. "She went into the Jamaican bakery. I waited a couple of doors down the street, but she never came out. She must have slipped out the back, because when I peeked in the window she wasn't inside."

"Did she steal something from the bakery?" Hector asked.

Lenni shrugged. "Didn't ask. I just ran over here."

"She must have spotted you," Alex said.

"Do you think we should follow her?" Gaby asked hesitantly. "In—in there?"

Tina gulped. "I don't like the idea of going into a boarded-up building."

"But we know she went in there," Jamal argued.

After a second Tina nodded. "If you guys are up for it, then I am too."

"I've got to find out what's up with Jade," Lenni insisted. "I'm going in!"

CHAPTER 9

Jamal, Tina, Gaby, Alex, and Hector followed Lenni up to the abandoned building. In front of the piece of metal that covered the doorway, Lenni hesitated. "This is really creepy," she muttered.

"I'll go first," Jamal volunteered. He pulled aside the metal sheet, which screeched faintly, and stepped through the dark opening.

Bang! "Ouch!" Jamal exclaimed.

"What happened?" Gaby whispered. She reached behind and grabbed Alex's arm.

"I stubbed my toe," Jamal answered. "Come on through. It's not so bad in here."

Cautiously the team members stepped inside the old building. Lenni gazed around the entrance hall. Enough daylight came through the boarded-up windows to show her that the hall, though very shabby, had been swept clean of trash and dirt. A staircase with a graceful wooden banister led up into blackness.

"Hey!" shouted a deep voice from the darkness above. Heavy footsteps descended toward the team.

"Yikes!" Gaby squeaked.

A huge man loomed up in front of Lenni and Jamal. He was well over six feet tall, with dark, longish hair and a heavy beard. He scowled angrily at the team. "This is no place for you! Get out!" he said.

Jamal backed away with Lenni beside him. "S-sorry," Jamal stuttered. "We—we were just looking for a friend. We thought she came in here."

"Her name's Jade Clintock. I go to school with her," Lenni added.

"You go to school with Jade?" the man asked, his voice softening.

Lenni nodded.

Suddenly the man broke into a smile. "Well, isn't that something!" he said. "I'm her father, Joshua Clintock. I'm glad to meet some of her friends."

"We never said we were her friends," Gaby whispered to Tina.

"Shh!" Tina said.

The man held out his hand. Lenni shook it. "My name's Lenni," she said. "Jade and I are teamed to do a history project together—"

"Project?" Mr. Clintock interrupted, looking puzzled.

"Project," Lenni repeated, "you know—for school?"

"Jade said nothing to me about a school project," Mr.

Clintock murmured, speaking as if to himself. "She never tells me anything anymore." Shaking his head, Mr. Clintock stepped aside. "Jade is up in her room. Won't you come in and wait?"

The kids on the team exchanged glances.

"Um—two of us will," Lenni agreed, grabbing Gaby's arm. She glanced at the rest of the team. "But my other friends will wait outside. We'll be back in a few minutes, guys."

As soon as the rest of the team left, Lenni and Gaby followed Joshua Clintock upstairs. In brownstone buildings like this one, Lenni knew, the living room was often on the second floor. Her heart was beating fast. What would they find up there? Did Jade really live here?

At the top of the stairs they passed a window that wasn't boarded up. Lenni peered through it. The one-story building in back of them had a skylight in the middle of its roof. Phil's workshop!

Mr. Clintock led Lenni into a large, bare room, furnished with only one old armchair and a kitchen chair, placed on either side of a fireplace in which there was a pile of odd-sized scraps of wood. In a corner of the room stood a stack of boards marked HAMMOND LUMBER. It was all Phil's wood, Lenni guessed.

"Are you building something?" she asked, pointing to the boards.

Joshua smiled. "Those are Jade's," he explained, his eyes roaming restlessly around the room as he spoke. "She's putting a bookshelf together. She's always working on something around the house—she's a good girl."

Lenni and Gaby exchanged glances. "Where did she get the wood?" Lenni tried to sound casual. Did Mr. Clintock know that his daughter stole? Did he encourage her to steal?

"I guess she picked it up somewhere," Joshua said vaguely. "Jade is clever at finding things."

"Oh," was all Lenni could think to say.

"Sit down," Mr. Clintock invited, waving his hand at the armchair.

Just then there came the sound of feet pounding down the stairs. "Dad, I'm going out for a while," came Jade's voice. "I'm going to get some—"

She stopped short as she came into the room and caught sight of Lenni and Gaby. After a second her eyes narrowed. "What are *you* doing here? You followed me, didn't you?"

"Jade, honey. That's not the way to talk to your friend," Joshua said gently.

"She's not a friend, Dad. She's just someone I know from school." Jade didn't look her father in the eye.

"Someone you're to do a project with?" Joshua asked.

"It's nothing," Jade said, her face turning red. "Just a stupid project." She glared at Lenni. "If you think I'm going to work with you after you followed me around and spied on me, you can forget it. I'm not doing any project with you, so you can just leave."

"Come, now," Joshua Clintock said. "Jade, you told me you were keeping up with your schoolwork."

"I am, don't worry," Jade said.

"Well, that's good," Mr. Clintock said, looking relieved.

· 70 ·

Lenni stared in disbelief. Max Frazier would never have let her get away with that!

Jade put her hands on her hips and glared at Lenni. "Why do you keep bothering me? Why can't you leave me alone?"

"I—I just wanted to help," Lenni said. "You seemed like you were in trouble and—"

"Trouble? What kind of trouble?" Joshua asked.

Jade stared tensely at Lenni. Lenni could tell she was waiting to see if Lenni would tell her father about the scene at Mr. Fernandez's store that morning.

But Lenni kept her mouth shut. *She* wasn't going to say anything.

"What kind of trouble? Jade, is something wrong?" Mr. Clintock pressed.

Suddenly Jade blew up. "Oh, wake up, Dad!" she shouted. "Look around you! We're homeless! We're living in an abandoned building! What do you mean, 'Is something wrong'!"

Lenni stood there in shocked silence. She couldn't believe how rudely Jade spoke to her own father. But she also couldn't believe how out of it Joshua Clintock was.

He seemed to shrink into his chair. "Times have been rough on us lately," he told Lenni and Gaby, as if they'd asked him for an explanation. "First Jade's mother was ill for so long. Then the bakery where I worked closed." Joshua shook his head slowly. "I had no work. Our savings all went to hospital bills. Then, right after Jade's mother died, we lost our house in a fire. So—"

"Here we are," Jade finished in a flat voice. She swung around on Lenni. "Now you know. Are you happy?"

Lenni swallowed. "I—I didn't mean to be nosy," she said. "Look, I guess we better go." She hesitated, then the words tumbled out in a rush. "Listen, Jade, you probably don't want me poking around, but—but you know where I hang if you—"

Jade turned away, her arms crossed over her chest.

"Never mind," Lenni said. "We've got to go."

"What happened?" Alex asked as soon as Lenni and Gaby came out of the building. "Are they really living there?"

Lenni didn't answer. She looked depressed.

"Well? Do they or don't they?" Alex asked. Tina nudged him with her elbow and shot him a look.

"Let's just go," Lenni said, shivering. "Hot chocolate at my house."

Soon they were in the Fraziers' cozy loft above the bodega, mugs of hot chocolate in their hands. Alex was bursting with questions. When he couldn't stand it any longer, he blurted out, "Lenni, tell us!"

"Yeah," Tina said. "Was everything okay in there?"

"Jade's father seemed"—Gaby lowered her voice—"you know, kind of spacy. Like he really didn't know what was going on."

"Really spacy," Tina added.

"Strange," Jamal corrected.

"It was creepy the way he seemed to look straight through us," Hector added.

Lenni looked down into her lap. "They've got problems. Her mom died, her dad's out of work, and they've got no real

home. They live there in that building. I don't know if they're even allowed to be there!"

"Man, that's rough," Hector said. "I can remember when my mom didn't have a job and she was trying to pay the rent. We needed help from my grandpa."

"Yeah, imagine if you didn't have any family to help you," Tina said. "When we came to America, we stayed with a cousin. If it hadn't been for him, my parents might never have saved enough to open their tailoring shop."

"What are we going to do?" Jamal asked. He got up and started pacing around. "I mean, Jade's really in trouble. How can we help?"

"Help?" Gaby said. "Jade's a thief. We should turn her in. She stole from our bodega and Phil's workshop. She broke the law!"

"Uh-uh, Gab," Alex said, shaking his head. "Remember, Mama and Papa had help when they first came to America. It's like Jade and her father just immigrated. They need help getting on their feet. They lost everything they had, just like Mama and Papa when they first came here. They have to start all over again too."

"But we didn't steal!" Gaby argued.

"You weren't even born yet, and I was just a baby," Alex reminded her. "We weren't old enough to steal!"

"Fine," Gaby muttered. She sat back against the wall away from the team as they continued talking. She'd seen where Jade lived and she felt sorry for the girl. But it wasn't fair that Jade was going to get away with stealing!

After a moment she pulled a pen and a small pad from her pocket and scribbled:

GHOSTWRITER, WE FOUND OUT THAT JADE AND HER FATHER LIVE IN AN ABANDONED BUILDING. HER FATHER DOESN'T HAVE A JOB. THEY DON'T EVEN HAVE MONEY TO BUY FOOD!

Ghostwriter wrote, **NOW IT MAKES SENSE THAT SHE WAS STEALING.**

Gaby frowned. YEAH, I GUESS, she wrote back. I FEEL BAD FOR JADE, BUT STEALING IS WRONG. SHE SHOULDN'T GET AWAY WITH WHAT SHE HAS DONE. WE WORK HARD AT THE BODEGA AND IT ISN'T FAIR THAT SHE CAN JUST TAKE THINGS.

WHAT DOES THE REST OF THE TEAM SAY? Ghostwriter wrote.

THEY DON'T WANT HER TO GET IN TROUBLE, Gaby wrote back. EVEN ALEX THINKS WE SHOULD HELP HER.

WHAT DO YOU WANT TO DO? Ghostwriter asked.

REPORT HER TO THE POLICE TO MAKE HER STOP STEALING, Gaby wrote. She considered for a second, then added: I THINK.

DID JADE NEED THE THINGS SHE STOLE? Ghostwriter questioned.

Gaby chewed on the pen cap for a while as she thought about the things Jade stole. Food to eat. Wood to keep warm and build furniture. Finally she wrote: MAYBE.

Closing her notebook, she moved closer to the rest of the team and listened to the conversation.

"So what are we going to do?" Hector asked.

"I don't know if we can do anything," Lenni finally said. "I don't think Jade wants us around."

"Poor Jade," Tina said. "It must be really hard with her father like that. It's almost like he's the kid and she's the parent."

Jamal shook his head. "Nobody should live like that."

"Yeah, but what can we do?" Alex asked.

"Well," Tina said, "Jade's dad needs a job. If he had a job he could buy food."

"And furniture," Hector threw in. "And a home."

"A home is hard to find," Lenni said thoughtfully. "Especially in New York. I wonder if we could help them find one?"

Alex looked excited. "Maybe we could!" he said. "People are always putting up signs in the bodega about rooms to rent and stuff. We could make some calls, check a few of them out."

"Mr. Clintock said he worked as a baker. I wonder if he can cook too. My dad's group has a lot of gigs in restaurants. Maybe one of them is looking for a cook," Lenni suggested. Her brown eyes were getting brighter. "I'll ask him to check around."

"Hey, maybe this won't be so hard after all!" Hector said enthusiastically.

Gaby had been silent all this time. Now Tina turned to her. "What do you think?" she asked.

"I want to help them too," Gaby said slowly, "but I still say it isn't right to steal. Jade may have needed the things she took, but it isn't fair to let her just get away with it."

Jamal nodded. "Gaby's right," he said quietly. "It would be wrong to let Jade off the hook."

"Well, maybe she can pay for some of the things she took," Tina answered. "Or find some other way to pay back what she can. Talk with your dad and see what he thinks."

"Okay," Gaby agreed, "I'll ask."

"I'll talk with Phil and see what he says too," Hector said. "Maybe if I tell him what we're doing, he'll want to help out also. You know, this is the season for giving and all."

Lenni was so excited, she felt like getting up and dancing. *Yeah,* she thought, *it is the season of giving. And we're going to give the Clintocks the best Christmas present they ever got—a whole new life!*

CHAPTER 10

"Man, I can't believe people are out shopping on a Sunday morning in this cold. They must have a lot of people to give presents to," Alex said, blowing on his chilled fingers. He and Hector stood on Myrtle Avenue giving out fliers. They'd been there all morning. But it was the last batch—Annette had promised!

As lunchtime approached, Alex's stomach began to rumble. "Hector, why don't we grab lunch right now? We can get a sandwich at the bodega," he suggested.

"I'm starved." Hector looked up and down the street at the mob of shoppers. "It's getting slow anyway."

Alex looked at Hector and laughed. "Right!" They shoved their fliers into a bag and headed for the bodega.

At the intersection Alex noticed a large billboard. He had seen it thousands of times before, but now it had a meaning it never had before. The billboard said:

Alex elbowed Hector to get his attention. "Hector," he said, "look." He pointed to the billboard.

"Yeah, so?"

"Jade and her dad live in an abandoned building," Alex said. "Maybe this organization can help them fix up their place and make it a real home."

"Hey!" Hector said, his eyes lighting up. He wrote the phone number onto a flier.

"I'll go after lunch," Alex suggested.

"Cool," Hector said. "Come on, I'm starving!"

"*Who* did you say stole my wood?" Phil said. He sounded shocked.

"Her name's Jade," Hector said. "She's a girl from the neighborhood." It was Hector's job to tell Phil about Jade and see if he could persuade Phil not to turn her in. Alex had gone to Urban Homesteaders.

Phil shook his head. "Why would a child steal wood?"

Hector stuck his hands deep into his jeans pockets to keep from fidgeting. "She lives with her dad in an abandoned building on the block," he explained. "They're . . . what-do-you-call-them . . . squatters. She took the wood for the fireplace."

"My cherry boards were used as firewood?" Phil yelled.

Hector gulped. "Not the boards. Lenni says Jade is using those to make a bookcase."

"That's one expensive bookcase," Phil replied. "You better get her to bring those boards back!"

"We will," Hector said. "We just wanted to ask you not to turn her in if she brings your wood back."

"Well . . . " Phil thought about it for a moment. "I guess nothing good would come out of reporting her."

Hector let out a sigh and headed for the door.

"Thanks, Phil, you won't be sorr—"

"Just a minute," Phil interrupted. "Not so fast."

Hector stopped in his tracks.

"I had to spend a lot of money because of Jade's break-ins," Phil said. "New locks. An alarm system."

Hector looked at Phil worriedly.

"I can live with not turning her in if she promises to help out at my workshop and Annette's place for a while." Phil folded his arms. "Sound fair?"

"Sounds great!" Hector agreed, relieved. "She'll even have fun working here!"

"We'll write up an agreement that says how long she'll have to work until everything is paid off. Maybe she can even help install the new lighting fixtures." Phil gave a half-smile. "I've decided to board up the skylight."

Hector grinned back a little nervously. Then he thought of something else. "I was wondering if you could tell me about how you fixed up your shop," he said.

Phil stroked his chin thoughtfully. "Well," he said, "I wanted my own place, but I couldn't afford to buy a building in the neighborhood. I used to walk by this old garage every day. The whole block was abandoned. Then one day I was on

Myrtle Avenue and I saw this billboard about an organization called—"

Hector snapped his fingers. "Urban Homesteaders!" he said at the same time as Phil.

"You must have seen the billboard too," Phil said, laughing. "They're a great group. They helped me find out how to buy this building from the city for a very good price. And they helped me get funding to fix it up."

Hector nodded. "Alex is over there right now trying to find out what we can do to help the Clintocks."

Phil patted Hector on the back. "That's great of you guys! I'm sure the Clintocks appreciate it."

"We haven't told them yet," Hector said excitedly. "It's a big surprise. Sort of a holiday present. Alex and I are going to find out how to rebuild their house, and Lenni's going to find a job for Mr. Clintock, and—"

"Whoa!" Phil cautioned, holding up his hands. "Careful not to bite off more than you can chew. Renovating a building is quite a project already."

"But they need money to pay for it, and to buy food and stuff," Hector argued. "If Mr. Clintock can just get a job, everything will be okay."

"Are you sure?" Phil asked. "It sounds to me like the Clintocks' problems might be bigger than that."

"Huh?" Hector said.

"It's a little hard to explain," Phil began. "But sometimes after a string of problems like the ones the Clintocks have had, people get kind of off-track."

Hector nodded, but he really didn't understand what Phil

was talking about. How could people have problems bigger than being homeless and jobless?

Just then Annette hurried through the door. "Ah, Hector!" she said as soon as she saw him. "How about handing out one last batch of fliers?"

"Sorry," Hector said hastily. "I was just leaving. See you later." Before Annette could answer, he backed out the door and headed for Urban Homesteaders.

Lenni and her father, Max Frazier, were eating lunch and watching the news on TV. A reporter was giving the weather forecast. Lenni wasn't interested—unless there was going to be a snowstorm and school would have to be canceled.

"Dad?"

"Hmm?"

Lenni took a deep breath. "I've got a friend at school who's been caught shoplifting."

Max sat up and clicked off the TV. "Which friend?"

"Someone you don't know. She was supposed to be my partner for this history project."

"And?"

"And, well, her dad lost his job and now they live in an abandoned building."

"That's awful," Max said.

Lenni's voice shook. "And her mom died last year."

Max nodded knowingly. His wife, Lenni's mother, had died when Lenni was seven.

"Jade seems so—so sad and angry all the time," Lenni added. "I think she needs help."

Max hugged Lenni to him, and for a while they sat silently.

"I know you want to help," Max finally said, "but what can you do?"

"Well, I was hoping that you could ask about cooking jobs at some of the places where you work, since Jade's dad used to be a baker," Lenni said eagerly.

"You want me to look around for job openings during my gigs? But, Bips, I don't have anything to do with the kitchen in these places," Max objected.

Lenni just looked at him. She knew her dad. If she waited long enough without saying anything, she could get him to come around and say yes.

"Restaurant managers can be kind of touchy," Max added. "So can chefs."

Lenni didn't budge.

"Oh, stop looking at me that way," Max said. "Say something."

"Please?"

Max sighed. "Okay. I'll see what I can do."

"Thanks! You're the best, Dad!" Lenni gave him a bear hug. She started to say something but Max cut her off.

"That's it," he said. "Don't even *think* of asking for any CDs!"

"Urban Homesteaders," Alex read aloud. He opened the door of the storefront building and went in.

Inside the shabby office a gray-haired woman with glasses was talking on the phone. Without interrupting her conversation she waved her hand at the seat in front of her desk. Alex sat down.

While the woman talked, Alex gazed at her bulletin board. It was full of cards and photos of people in their new homes. One of the photos was of Phil in his workshop. He had on his work smock and was drilling a screw into the wall.

Finally the woman hung up. "Yes, may I help you?" she asked.

"That's Phil!" Alex said, pointing to the photo.

"Why, yes," the woman said, sounding surprised. "Are you a friend of his?"

"He's helping me make a bookcase for my sister."

"That's nice," she said. "I'm glad his shop is doing well. It wasn't so long ago that he was sitting right there." She pointed her pencil at Alex.

"Really? You mean you helped him?"

Suddenly the door flew open and Hector appeared. "Alex!" he panted. "Phil got his shop through these guys!"

"I just found out," Alex said, pointing to the photo. He turned to the woman. "This is Hector."

The woman smiled, and reached across to shake Hector's hand. "Hi, there, I'm—"

"Rachel Howard," Hector said. "Phil told me already."

"Oh," she said with a laugh. "Then we'd better get down to business. How can I help you?"

"We'd like to find out about how to take over an abandoned building," Alex said.

Ms. Howard raised an eyebrow. "Is this a school project?"

"It's for a friend," Hector said.

"Well, kind of the father of a friend," Alex added quickly.

"And where is the building?"

"Over on Waverly, just off Clinton," Alex answered.

"I know the block," Ms. Howard said, nodding. "I've had my eye on those buildings for a while. The city was going to tear them down and put up an office block, but they ran out of money. Now they're just sitting there."

"I knew it was a good spot!" Hector said excitedly.

"It is," Ms. Howard agreed. "Now, before we do anything, you need to bring your friend in so that I can find out what kind of help he qualifies for."

"Um," Alex said. He and Hector glanced at each other. The only thing was, they were going to have to tell Joshua Clintock first. It would ruin the surprise!

"Hello!" Lenni called. "Anyone home?"

She, Alex, Jamal, Tina, Gaby, and Hector were in the hallway of Jade and Joshua Clintock's abandoned building. When a deep voice answered, they climbed the steps.

In the barren living room they saw Joshua Clintock kneeling by a board covered with wet plaster. He was decorating it with bottle caps and colored glass. His clothes were covered with white dust.

"Hi, Mr. Clintock," Lenni said. "We've got some stuff to show you. A kind of surprise."

"Come in, come in," Mr. Clintock said. He pointed at the plaster-covered board. "What do you think?"

"It's really neat," Hector said.

"I like the swirls," Tina said. "It reminds me of waves at the beach."

"Yeah," Jamal agreed. "Are you going to try to sell it?"

"Oh, no," Mr. Clintock said. He stuck another soda cap into the wet plaster. "Sell it? No. It's for Jade."

Lenni couldn't stand the suspense anymore. She had to tell him all the good news! "Mr. Clintock," she said, "we think we can help."

"Help?" Mr. Clintock echoed. "What do you mean?"

"We've been checking around," Jamal said, "and we have some information for you."

"I've got a lead on a job," Lenni bubbled. "All you have to do is talk to the manager of this club where my dad plays. He said he can see you tomorrow night."

Mr. Clintock looked alarmed. "Tomorrow?"

"Yeah, and we found out about this organization that will help you fix up this building, make it a real home." Hector held out a pamphlet from Urban Homesteaders.

Mr. Clintock stepped back as if Hector were holding a gun.

"It's okay," Alex said. "They're cool. Our friend Phil has a woodworking shop that he renovated with Urban Home-steaders. You can talk to him if you want to."

"But I . . . oh, my," Joshua Clintock said, shaking his head. He paced to the other side of the room, then back, then away again.

Lenni and Jamal exchanged glances. Was something wrong?

"Just imagine what this place will look like once you finish renovating," Tina said.

"Maybe," Gaby muttered, looking around at the mess.

"Oh, my," Joshua Clintock said again.

Lenni beamed. He must be so happy, he didn't know what to say!

Mr. Clintock looked at his feet. "I'm not sure," he said, putting a hand to his lips. "Tomorrow? I don't think I can make it. I have too much to do."

"Like what?" Gaby burst out.

Lenni stared at him, shocked and confused. He sounded as if he didn't really *want* to apply for a job!

Suddenly feet thumped up the steps, two at a time. Jade burst into the room, then stopped abruptly, her gaze roaming over the team.

Finally her eyes settled on Lenni. They narrowed angrily. "I told you to stay out of my life!"

"Now, Jade," Mr. Clintock said. "Don't be rude. Your friends are only trying to help." He sat down abruptly and clenched his hands in his lap. "They say they've found me a job and a way for us to have a home again."

"Get real, Dad," Jade said scornfully. She threw her knapsack on the floor.

"But it's true!" Lenni said eagerly. "I found an interview for your dad, and—"

Jade's face turned pale. "You did what? Why are you messing with our lives? It's none of your business! Didn't you hear me last time?"

"Wait," Jamal said, but Jade cut him off too.

· 88 ·

"I can take care of us! I don't need your help!" Jade yelled.

"Jade, we only—" Lenni started to say.

"Get out!" Jade kicked a chair across the floor. "Get out! Get out of our lives! No one wants you here!"

Tina grabbed Lenni's arm.

"But, Jade," Joshua Clintock said faintly. Jade glared at her father. He sank back in his chair.

Jade faced the team again. "I don't need you. Any of you!" she yelled. Whirling, she ran out of the room and thudded up the stairs.

CHAPTER 11

No one knew what to say.

"I'm sorry," Joshua finally said. He leaned back and closed his eyes, shaking his head.

"Come on," Jamal said to Lenni, taking her hand. Silently everyone left.

"Let's stop in at Joe's Pizza," Jamal suggested as they walked outside. "I could use a soda—and we need to talk. And maybe we should get Ghostwriter in on this."

Everyone agreed and the kids headed down the street.

When they were seated at a booth, Lenni took out a pen and wrote in her notebook:

GHOSTWRITER, I MESSED UP EVERYTHING!

WHAT HAPPENED? Ghostwriter asked.

I DON'T EVEN KNOW! Lenni wrote.

Alex put his arm around Lenni's shoulders. "It wasn't your fault."

"We just wanted to help," Hector added.

WE WANTED TO MAKE EVERYTHING BETTER FOR JADE AND HER DAD, Lenni explained. WE GOT HIM A JOB INTERVIEW AND A WAY TO FIX UP THEIR PLACE INTO A REAL HOME. IT WAS LIKE A PRESENT.

SO WHAT'S WRONG? Ghostwriter wrote back.

IT DIDN'T WORK OUT THE WAY WE THOUGHT IT WOULD. JADE GOT SO MAD. SHE SAID SHE DIDN'T NEED HELP. IT'S LIKE SHE WANTS TO PRETEND EVERYTHING IS OKAY WITH THEIR LIVES.

WHY? Ghostwriter wrote.

Lenni thought about that. After a moment she said slowly, thinking aloud, "Jade didn't want anyone to know that she was homeless."

"And it was almost like she was trying to protect her father from us," Alex added. "Like Tina said—it's like she's the parent and he's the child."

Jamal nodded. "I see what you mean. Maybe—maybe that's why our helping hurt her so much."

"We saw what she didn't want us to see," Tina added softly.

"When I talked to Phil," Hector said, "he told me that maybe the Clintocks had bigger problems than being homeless and poor. I think maybe now I know what he was talking about. Mr. Clintock isn't ready for a job."

"Kids," the pizza man called from the counter, "if you're not going to eat, I need that table."

"We're going," Gaby called. The group stood up and moved back out into the cold December afternoon.

Lenni heaved a deep sigh. "We really messed up this time."

"We didn't know, Lenni," Tina said. "Helping someone isn't always such a terrible thing."

"I don't get it," Gaby burst out. "Why should we feel bad? I figured Jade would be psyched."

"Gaby," Alex said, "maybe we did too much figuring without thinking about how the Clintocks might feel."

"Yeah," Jamal agreed. "I think they both know her father can't handle a job right now—but they never had to face it until we shoved one in front of him. I think maybe they need to find their own way back."

After a moment Gaby nodded.

The team was halfway down the block when, suddenly, the harsh jangling of a burglar alarm split the air.

"What's that?" Hector cried. "It sounds like it's coming from—"

"Oh, no," Alex said, breaking into a run. "It's coming from Phil's workshop!"

They all raced as fast as they could toward Phil's shop. They dashed inside just as the alarm cut off.

Phil was striding toward the table saw. "Drop that!" he yelled.

Lenni gasped. Jade stood on the table saw, her arms loaded with Phil's tools. Shattered glass from the skylight had spread across the floor.

"The police are on their way," Phil said firmly. "Drop the stuff and get down."

"Jade!" Lenni said.

Jade's face slowly flushed red, but she didn't look at the team.

"Oh, so this is the girl who's been breaking into my shop and stealing my wood. This is how she thanks me for not reporting her to the police?" Phil said, turning to Hector. He shook his head. "Smashing the skylight in broad daylight! Not good! I don't see that I have any choice but to turn her in now."

"Wait!" Lenni took a step forward. "It's not her fault—well, maybe it is her fault. But she was mad at us. Please don't turn her in!"

"Shut up!" Jade hissed. "Why are you doing this? What do you want from me?"

Lenni stared at her, bewildered. "I don't want anything from you," she said. "I'm just trying to help."

Suddenly Jade's face seemed to crumple and she burst into tears. "I just had to—I had to do something," she sobbed. "I had to!"

Phil frowned. "It almost sounds as if you didn't care about getting caught."

Jade sobbed harder.

Outside, a siren from a police car drew closer. Hector tugged at Phil's sleeve.

"Please, Phil, don't turn her in," he whispered.

"Maybe you could talk to her dad," Gaby added.

Alex put an arm around his sister's shoulders. "Now you're talking!"

Phil took Jade by the arm and helped her to the floor. They stared at each other.

"Listen, I won't turn you in," he said after a second. "But no more breaking in. And no more stealing. Got it?"

Jade nodded tensely.

The police car pulled up to the shop. Two officers hopped out and entered. Everyone held their breath.

"Sorry, fellas. It was just a false alarm," Phil said, waving his hand in a friendly gesture.

"All okay?" one of the officers asked, glancing at the shattered glass. "What about that window?" He pointed to the skylight.

"A piece of wood shot up from the saw," Phil answered. "The kids were fooling around."

"We'll make it up to you," Hector said, playing into Phil's story. "Promise!"

The second officer peered at Jade's tearstained face, then shrugged. "Whatever you say."

"Thanks anyway," Phil said.

When they were gone, Phil turned to Jade. "Now, where do you live? I want to talk to your father."

Jade's eyes filled again. She gazed around at the team. "Will you—will you guys come with us?" she whispered.

Lenni swallowed and nodded. "Sure."

Everyone marched out of the workshop and around the block to the brownstone where Jade and her father lived.

Inside the abandoned building Mr. Clintock was still sitting in his chair with a hand covering his eyes. He started as everyone trooped into the room.

"What's going on?" he asked.

"My name's Phil Reiner. I just caught your daughter breaking into my workshop," Phil said.

Mr. Clintock wrinkled his forehead. "What? My Jade? No, you've made a mistake."

"No mistake," Phil said. "And it's not the first time either."

Joshua Clintock stared at his daughter. "Jade?"

Jade looked away. "I'm sorry," she said.

Mr. Clintock's shoulder's sagged. But Lenni, watching him, thought that he didn't really look all that surprised.

After a moment he lifted his head and looked straight at Phil. "I'm terribly sorry," he said. There was a sudden firmness in his voice that Lenni and her friends had never heard before.

"Well, that's fine, but you'll have to replace everything she took. And broke," Phil added. "She broke through the skylight this time."

"Of course," Mr. Clintock said. "And—Mr. Reiner? This won't happen again. I won't let it. Things have gone too far!"

Everyone was staring at Mr. Clintock as he stood up. "Lenni, when was that interview you told me about?"

"Tomorrow—Monday," Lenni answered. "Nine P.M."

"Fine." Mr. Clintock patted some dust from his clothes. "I'd appreciate it if you'd ask your father to say I'll be there promptly at nine."

A grin spread across Lenni's face. "You got it!"

"Dad!" Jade flew to her father's side and flung her arms around him.

He hugged her to him for a long moment. Then he turned to Phil. "Now, Mr. Reiner," he said, "would you be so good as to estimate how much we owe you?"

As Phil started ticking off items on his fingers, Lenni beckoned to the team. "Let's go," she whispered. "They've got work to do!"

"I don't get it," Gaby complained softly as they went down the stairs. "What happened to Mr. Clintock? It's like he suddenly turned into a different person!"

"I'm not sure," Lenni said. "But I think it's what Jamal said. I think maybe the Clintocks are starting to find their own way back!"

On Tuesday, Lenni paced the floor anxiously. It was 5:10, and Jade was late. "She isn't going to show," Lenni muttered. "I should have known."

In front of her was an almost empty tray of cookies. They were double chocolate chunk, her favorite.

"Oh, well," Lenni said. She picked up the last one and was about to stuff it into her mouth when the bell rang. She ran to open the door. Jade stood in the hall.

"Oh, hi! Uh, come in." Lenni wasn't sure what to say. She held out the last cookie to Jade.

Jade took it. "I love this kind," she said.

"Me too," Lenni said, showing Jade the empty tray. "Sorry."

Jade giggled. After a second Lenni started to chuckle too. Soon they were both cracking up.

Finally they calmed down. Jade looked almost shyly at Lenni. "Guess what," she said. "My dad got that job."

"Really?"

Jade smiled.

"Yes!" Lenni said. She held up her hand and slapped Jade's palm. "That's kickin'!"

"Yeah!" Jade's smile grew even broader.

There was a pause. "So, um, you want to start working on our project?" Jade asked finally.

"Sit right down," Lenni said, pointing at the couch. "I was about to give up!"

"There still are three whole days," Jade said.

"Easy for you to say!" Lenni said. She snapped her fingers as she remembered something. "Before we start, though, I've got something for you." She dug into the "everything" drawer in the kitchen and grabbed the embroidered glove. "Here," she said, handing it to Jade.

"My glove!" Jade gasped.

"Hector found it in Phil's shop," Lenni said.

"I thought I had lost it forever!" Suddenly Jade frowned. "How did you know it was mine?"

"Uh . . ." Lenni couldn't tell Jade about Ghostwriter! "We have our ways," she answered instead, wiggling her eyebrows.

Jade slipped the glove onto her hand. "My mom made these for me before she died," she said in a soft voice. "She embroidered them with a line from her favorite poem."

"Half on one glove, half on the other," Lenni said, nodding.

"Right!" Another smile lit Jade's face. "My mom used to say it reminded her of me. 'Two roads diverged in a wood, and I—' "

" 'I took the one less traveled by,' " Lenni finished.

"You know it?"

Lenni nodded. "I do now."

"Mom used to say that I always took the hard way," Jade said.

At that Lenni had to laugh. "You do, Jade," she agreed. "You really do!"

EPILOGUE

It was a June afternoon, and the once-abandoned brown-stone around the corner from Phil's shop was alive with activity. Lenni was painting trim around the dining-room door. Hector was helping Phil install a wood counter in the kitchen. Alex, Jamal, Gaby, and Tina were painting the walls.

Jade stood on a stepladder wiping the new windows. Her father walked over and inspected them, then nodded.

"These will keep out the drafts," he said, sounding pleased. "It shouldn't cost too much to heat this place. And with my job at the Regina Bakery I'll have the money to install a boiler before winter."

"Alex, you're getting more paint on you than the walls," Gaby scolded.

Alex dabbed paint onto Gaby's nose with his finger.

"Alex!" Gaby yelled.

"Oops," Alex said as he jumped out of Gaby's reach. "You look like a white-nosed Rudolph."

"Chill out," Jamal said, but Hector was already rolling on the floor, he thought Alex was so funny, and Jamal couldn't help but laugh a little too.

"I'm just about done," Lenni called.

"Us too," Jamal said. He ran his paint roller over the last bare spot of wall. "There!"

"Finished!" everyone yelled.

Mr. Clintock beamed down from a ladder, where he was attaching a light fixture to the ceiling. "It looks great!" he said. "You kids ought to start a renovation business." His voice grew softer. "I can't thank you enough. You've done so much for us!"

"Yo, Hector, do you have that stuff we talked about?" Lenni said.

"I'll go get it," Hector said.

"I'll help," Tina said. She and Hector ran down the stairs.

"What stuff?" Jade asked.

"Just a little housewarming present," Alex said.

"It's not so little!" Gaby objected. The gift had been her idea. "You couldn't carry it all by yourself!"

"What is it?" Jade asked. Her eyes were shining.

"You'll see," Jamal said, grinning.

"No, tell me!" Jade said. "You have to!"

"Chill out." Lenni laughed. "It's here now!"

Everyone gathered in the living room.

"Tah-dah!" Hector said as he and Tina appeared in the

doorway. Between them was a bookcase like the one Alex and Hector had made for Gaby.

"Oh, my!" Mr. Clintock said, beaming.

"You guys made that?" Jade asked. "For us?"

"Well, we know you like to read," Lenni said.

"Phil let us use his workshop again," Hector said.

"It's beautiful. We'll cherish it," Mr. Clintock said.

"There's one more thing," Lenni said. "The bookcase looked kind of lonely with no books on it." She smiled and looked at the rest of the team. "So we thought we'd start you off." She handed Jade a package.

Jade quickly tore it open and read out loud: *"The Poetry of Robert Frost."* She hugged the book to her.

"Thanks," she said. There were tears in her eyes as she looked around at the team members. "Thanks!"

Alex shuffled his feet. "No big deal," he muttered, embarrassed.

Jade smiled. "I just wish I had something for you guys too."

Lenni rolled her eyes. "You've already helped me pass history!" she said. "How else could I have made an A-minus on that paper?"

Everyone laughed.

Jamal took the book and opened it to a poem. "Have you guys read this?" he asked his friends. "It's pretty cool. Listen."

Everyone was silent as he read the poem aloud. When Jamal reached the last line, Ghostwriter's glow appeared on the page. He picked up letters from the poem and flung them into

a shimmering message in the air. The kids on the team hid their smiles as they read the words no one else could see:

THIS TIME YOU MADE ALL THE DIFFERENCE, TEAM!

From the
Hit TV Show
Ghost writer

Created by CTW

BECOME AN OFFICIAL
GHOSTWRITER READERS CLUB MEMBER!

You'll receive the following GHOSTWRITER Readers Club Materials:
Official Membership Card • The Scoop on GHOSTWRITER •
GHOSTWRITER Magazine

All members registered by December 31st will have a chance to win
a FREE COMPUTER and other exciting prizes!

OFFICIAL ENTRY FORM

Mail your completed entry to: Bantam Doubleday Dell BFYR,
GW Club, 1540 Broadway, New York, NY 10036

Name _____

Address _____

City _____ **State** _____ **Zip** _____

Date of birth _____ **Phone** _____

Club Sweepstakes Official Rules
1. No purchase necessary. Enter by completing and returning the Entry Coupon. All entries must be received by Bantam
   Doubleday Dell no later than December 31, 1993. No mechanically reproduced entries allowed. By entering the
   sweepstakes, each entrant agrees to be bound by these rules and the decision of the judges which shall be final and binding.
   Limit: one entry per person.
2. The prizes are as follows: Grand Prize: One computer with monitor (approximate retail value of Grand Prize $3,000), First
   Prizes: Ten GHOSTWRITER libraries (approximate retail value of each First Prize: $25), Second Prizes: Five GHOSTWRITER
   backpacks (approximate retail value of each Second Prize: $25), and Third Prizes: Ten GHOSTWRITER T-shirts (approximate
   retail value of each Third Prize: $10). Winners will be chosen in a random drawing on or about January 10, 1994, from
   among all completed Entry Coupons received and will be notified by mail. Odds of winning depend on the number of
   entries received. No substitution or transfer of the prize is allowed. All entries become property of BDD and will not be
   returned. Taxes, if any, are the sole responsibility of the winner. BDD reserves the right to substitute a prize of equal or
   greater value if any prize becomes unavailable.
3. This sweepstakes is open only to the residents of the U.S. and Canada, excluding the Province of Quebec, who are between
   the ages of 6 and 14 at the time of entry. The winner, if Canadian, will be required to answer correctly a time-limited
   arithmetical skill testing question in order to receive the prize. Employees of Bantam Doubleday Dell Publishing Group Inc.
   and its subsidiaries and affiliates and their immediate family members are not eligible. Void where prohibited or restricted
   by law. Grand and first prize winners will be required to execute and return within 14 days of notification an affidavit of
   eligibility and release to be signed by winner and winner's parent or legal guardian. In the event of noncompliance with
   this time period, an alternate winner will be chosen.
4. Entering the sweepstakes constitutes permission for use of the winner's name, likeness, and biographical data for publicity
   and promotional purposes on behalf of BDD, with no additional compensation. For the name of the winner, available after
   January 31, 1994, send a self-addressed envelope, entirely separate from your entry, to Bantam Doubleday Dell, BFYR
   Marketing Department, 1540 Broadway, New York, NY 10036.

From the
Hit TV Show

Ghost writer

Created by CTW

GHOSTWRITER—READ IT! SOLVE IT! TELL A FRIEND! CHECK OUT THESE GHOSTWRITER BOOKS.

❑ A Match of Wills	29934-4	$2.99/3.50 Can.
❑ Courting Danger and other Stories	48070-7	$2.99/3.50 Can.
❑ Dress Code Mess	48071-5	$2.99/3.50 Can.
❑ The Ghostwriter Detective Guide	48069-3	$2.99/3.50 Can.
❑ The Big Book of Kids' Puzzles	37074-X	$1.25/1.50 Can.
❑ The Mini Book of Kids' Puzzles	37073-1	$1.25/1.50 Can.
❑ Off the Top of Your Head	37157-6	$1.25/1.50 Can.
❑ Steer Clear of Haunted Hill	48087-1	$2.99/3.50 Can.
❑ Alias Diamond Jones	37216-5	$2.99/3.50 Can.
❑ Doubletalk: Codes, Signs and Symbols	37218-1	$1.25/1.50 Can.
❑ Rally!	48092-8	$3.50/3.99 Can.
❑ Blackout!	37302-1	$2.99/3.50 Can.

Bantam Doubleday Dell
Books for Young Readers

Bantam Doubleday Dell
Dept. DA 60
2451 South Wolf Road
Des Plaines, IL 60018

Please send the items I have checked above. I am enclosing $_____ (please add $2.50 to cover postage and handling). Send check or money order, no cash or C.O.D.s please.

Name _____

Address _____

City _____ State _____ Zip _____

Please allow four to six weeks for delivery.
Prices and availability subject to change without notice.   DA 60 2/94